Personal Foul

Rangers Football
Book 3

Kameron Claire

Snuggle Whore Press, LLC

To all the Witty, Wicked & Wild Readers...
Never let them silence our Witty tongues,
Never let them shame our Wicked needs,
Never let them stop our Wild deeds.

Thank you for the love and support!

ROCKY MOUNTAIN
RANGERS

Chapter One
Aggie

"We are partying tonight!" Rex calls across the locker room. He's joined by a series of hoots and hollers.

"Strip club!" Jepson bellows.

"You got us kicked out of the last strip club, remember?" Rex says.

"That was in Nashville. We have a dozen other cities to be kicked out of this year and besides, the ladies at Diamonds and Pearls love me." Jepson grins as he yanks off his jersey, his chest smooth and clean compared to his twin brother's which is marked by scars and tattoos.

"What do you say, Ags? Are you ready for a night out on the town? We can bust your strip club cherry." Devlin bumps me on the shoulder. He's one of the best receivers in the league and also one of the nicest guys I know. I'm currently living in his basement while I wait for my divorce to be complete, my soon-to-be-ex taking everything, including the house and my dog.

I grimace. "Strip club? It feels juvenile, man."

"Yeah, it is. But it's also a rite of passage you should have experienced years ago."

"My divorce isn't final yet." I grab my toiletry kit and follow him to the showers.

He shrugs. "So? It's not like you're getting back together with her, right?"

"No, of course not, but you know how Ellen is. If she finds out I went to a strip club, she'll figure out a way to use that information against me in the divorce." I can't wait to get to the other side of this and start the next phase of my life where I'm not afraid of a five-foot-four weasel full of piss and vinegar.

Looking at myself from the outside, I'm disgusted by the man I've become. Timid, gun shy, beaten—I'm too tired to fight her and yet that's the only option I have. All I want is the life I deserve—no more and no less. I'm a good man, even though she's told me otherwise for over ten years.

Now I just need to believe it.

"It's not illegal for married men to frequent strip clubs, Aggie. Hell, some guys' wives go with their husbands and get their own lap dances."

"Yeah, but Ellen is not one of them. At least she wasn't with me."

"No." He shakes his head. "Not with you."

We both know what he means by that statement. He's the one that had to break to me the rumor that Ellen was screwing Patrick Deming, a third-string defensive lineman from our team. At least half the team knew about the affair by the time I found out.

Freaking humiliating.

I grab a shower stall and wash off the sweat worked up during a hard-played, amazing game. Our quarterback, Declan Scott, broke personal and league records, which means my teammates and I played near perfectly, providing him with the protection he needed to get the ball into the end zone four times against the fourth toughest defense in the league.

"Aggie." Greg Millen, the offensive coordinator, is standing outside the showers with his hand on the back of his neck and eyes down to the ground.

I turn off the water and poke my head out of the stall. "Coach?"

"Get dressed. Grab your stuff. You need to follow me upstairs."

"Am I in trouble?" I secure a towel around my waist and walk toward him.

"I don't know, man, but they're waiting for us." Greg shakes his head and turns on his heel, projecting his voice into the locker room loud with a post-game high. "No one leaves until the coach and the GM talk to you. Rex, do you hear me?"

"Yeah, Coach," Rex grumbles.

Greg nods. "I'll meet you at the front door, Aggie."

I slump down in front of my locker, making quick work of packing my duffel bag. My heart sinks into my belly, a familiar feeling over the last couple of months.

God knows what kind of trouble I'm in now, but I don't seem to be able to avoid it no matter what I do.

"What's going on, man?" Devlin asks.

"I don't know." I sigh. "They called me upstairs."

He shrugs. "Don't sweat it, baby. Maybe they want to pay you a bonus or something for the game today. You were amazing."

"Getting good news isn't part of my life lately," I mutter, trying not to be a downer. He doesn't deserve my negativity, especially tonight when he also broke his personal receiving record. He should celebrate with everyone else.

"Shit is about to turn around for you. I promise." He smacks my shoulder. "You need a ride to the house?"

Right now, I don't even have my car. Ellen took it, and I haven't taken the time to fight with her about it. Her lawyer got me kicked out of my house even though I'm the one who filed a restraining order against her. She kept the keys to all three of our cars, so I have no wheels and have been driving Devlin's extra car when I need to.

Of course, we drove together today since we're playing at home.

"No. I don't want you waiting around for me since I don't know how long I'll be. I'll grab a Lyft or something."

"Alright, man. I'll have food waiting for you when you get home."

"Thanks, brother." I pull my T-shirt on over my head, stand and slide my joggers up, regretting I don't have a suit in my locker.

Although, getting fired in scrubby clothes seems fitting, given my life as of late.

I follow Greg to the elevators and ride up to the fourth floor and executive offices. We enter a conference room between the president's and general manager's offices, one wall a solid bank of windows overlooking a darkening stadium. Sitting across a massive wooden conference room table is the team's lawyer, Mr. Paul Mendelssohn, Esq. and the president of team communications, Ms. Deidre Scott—who stops mid-conversation to look at me with a hard, scrutinizing expression on her otherwise beautiful face.

"Dang," I murmur, glancing down at my crappy clothes. I make eleven million dollars a year, but with my accounts frozen and Ellen setting fire to my clothes after I served her papers, I'm down to the bare necessities.

Of course, I have to look like shit in front of her. The heiress to the Scott family fortune and toughest woman in football, Deidre Scott could have been a lingerie model, but chose to be the organization's—as well as the family's—marketing and communication executive.

Not that I've fantasized about seeing her in her underwear, because that would be so damn inappropriate I'd have to pray nightly for strength and forgiveness.

So yeah, lead me not into temptation and all that—I'm well acquainted.

She's by far the most beautiful woman I've ever met face to face, as well as the smartest, but in some ways, she's also the scariest. She's no bullshit and has a reputation for making grown men cuss and cry if they cross her or the family.

I've heard her brother call her Buster, short for ball-buster and from the rumors, it's an apropos nickname.

I wonder why she is here?

"Have a seat, Mr. Dunham." She arches her brow and points to the chair at the end of the table, farthest from her. "Greg, you should be with the team when Dad talks to them. They just left the press junket and are walking that way now."

"Okay." Greg gives my upper arm a squeeze before walking out and closing the door behind him.

I take the seat, racking my brain on what I could have done to get myself called into the big office. Yes, I have a lot of personal drama going on. I filed for divorce four months ago, but considering Ellen is contesting, it's still not final. I've had a restraining order against her since a mediation meeting went horribly wrong and she set my clothes on fire ten weeks ago.

That night, she invited me to the house wearing a babydoll nightie, one I would have gone gaga over a year ago. I'm a simple man, and she's spent our entire relation-ship gaslighting me and using sex as a weapon. Ellen isn't used to hearing me say no. I'm a peacekeeper and have cowered to her since the day we met, but that evening I not only told her no, I said hell no and never again.

That pissed her off.

Her behavior follows a pattern. She's physically and verbally abusive, throwing a tantrum over one thing or another and then later seduces me with a half-ass apology and a night of sex. It's a pattern we've followed for nearly twelve years. She's also the only woman I've ever been with. We lost our virginity to each other and yet, as it turns out, I'm not the only man she's been with by a long shot.

Learned that six months ago. Although, if I think back, I should have known all along.

I know I'm a big sucker, but I believe in keeping promises and I vowed to love, honor and cherish her until death do us part.

However, even that vow was built on a lie.

Devlin, along with a couple of other players on the team, finally convinced me that those vows don't mean shit if both parties aren't adhering to them.

Ellen doesn't want a divorce, even though I caught her cheating on me with not one, but two different guys—and those are just the ones I know about with absolutely surety. To say I am humiliated is an understatement. I've bent over backwards for her since we were eight years old, not because I was head-over-heels in love, but because she was the first person to tell me I was special. According to her, it was us against the world, only I never realized she was the one pushing everyone away, including my family. It has always been rocky, but considering we're from a small aging town with less than a hundred school-age kids, we were all each other had. We had to take the bus over an hour to go to middle school, and I was driving illegally at fourteen so I could attend football practice—our only ticket out of Rizona, Texas.

It was either football or the military.

Then, right before we graduated high school, Ellen told me she was pregnant. We got married before I left for training camp at Texas A&M, where I had earned a full-ride scholarship. By the end of the summer, she'd had a miscarriage, or so she said. Only later did I learn she'd lied about the pregnancy. She was positive that if I left her behind for college, I would've met another woman and broken up with her.

In retrospect, I'm sure she was right. I'd like to believe time apart would've made me realize how manipulative of a person Ellen is, but instead I entered college as a married man and never reflected on my sheltered, gaslit life. We lived in an apartment off campus. She worked while I went to class, trained, and played football.

And that, in a nutshell, has been my life. Football and Ellen and nothing else.

Daniel, Deacon and Declan Scott walk in with our head coach, Mike Monroe. Declan immediately comes to my side, putting a hand on my shoulder. "You okay?"

"I don't know what's going on," I say under my breath.

"Seriously?" His head snaps up to look at his sister. "Buster? You didn't tell him why he's here?"

She narrows her eyes. "It's not my place, Declan. That would be the GM or operations manager or even the coach's job."

"Deidre." Daniel Scott, the GM and family patriarch, shakes his head and sighs before taking a seat to the right of me. Declan sits on the other side while Deacon shakes my hand before sitting next to his father.

"Am I fired?" I say, since no one is telling me what's going on.

"I hope not, son," Daniel says with a somber note.

Deidre taps on a tablet in her hand and a picture of Ellen, bruised and bloodied, appears on the big screen across the room.

"What the hell?" I suck in my breath, my pulse speeding up. "What happened? Was she in an accident? Is she okay?"

"Did you do it?" Deidre raises her brow. "Did you beat your wife?"

"What?!?" I jump out of my seat and push back from the table, shaking my head hard as I have something akin to an out-of-body experience. This isn't happening. This can't be f-ing happening. "I didn't lay a hand on her. Believe me, Coach."

Declan also stands. "No one is accusing you, Aggie. Right, Deidre?"

She crosses her arms over her chest and narrows her gaze on me but says nothing.

"Deidre!" Declan snaps.

Her eyes never leave me as she ignores her brother's outburst. "Look me in the eye and say you don't beat women."

I rarely hold direct eye contact with women because of my size—I don't want to intimidate them with an aggressive stare on top of everything else, but for this conversation I bring my eyes up to hers and hold my ground. "I don't hit women, Ms. Scott. Ellen has hit me many times, but I've never so much as pushed her away from me, much less laid an open palm on her."

"It's true. We've all seen her swing at him when she gets in a mood." Declan backs me up.

"Sorry, Aggie." Deidre relaxes her shoulders. "I had to be absolutely sure it wasn't true. Since I'll be the one spinning this story for the media, I need your raw reaction to the allegation."

"Media?"

"I have contacts inside SMZ who sent me these images so we can get ahead of the story. Ellen emailed them to a producer with a claim that you beat and raped her two nights ago."

I'm too shocked to speak.

Zapped of the last of my emotional energy, I slump down into a chair. I can't defeat her. Ellen is too good at lying, forming mean girl cliques and plotting vicious attacks. I shake my head and say again, "Am I fired?"

"No, Aggie. We're not letting one of the best offensive lineman in the league go," Deacon says, standing and once again smacking my shoulder.

"Have you had any contact with her since you put the protective order in place?" Paul asks.

I shake my head. "No. I haven't even accepted a phone call and trust me, my cell rings twenty-four-seven. She's shown up at Devlin's door multiple times, but luckily, he's dealt with her by calling the neighborhood's private security."

Deidre grabs the tablet and closes the image, the big

screen thankfully going black. "Paul and I can handle it from here, but Aggie, we're going to have to get personal with you. I really am sorry, but there's no other way."

"I'll tell you anything you want to know, but what's the point? She'll never give up until she's taken everything and sends me back to the trailer."

"We're not going to let that happen." Deidre arches her brow. "You're a Ranger, and we take care of our own."

Daniel stands with Deacon and Declan, nodding toward the door. "We'll leave it to you, Deidre. Clean this up."

"Yeah, I need this guy protecting me on the field." Declan grips my shoulders and gives a reassuring squeeze.

"I'm all over it." Deidre smiles, and I swear, there's a twinkle in her eye as if she's looking forward to the fight.

Everyone leaves the conference room except Paul and Deidre. "Let's move this into my office. It's a little less formal, and there's alcohol which I think we could all use a shot of."

Chapter Two
Deidre

Arnold Aggie Dunham is a big man, and that's coming from a six-foot tall woman who regularly wears four-inch heels to stand near eye to eye with her two massive brothers. The media will have a field day using Aggie's size against him as they paint him as a misogynistic abuser, if I can't stop them before they start their onslaught.

But one look at Aggie as he follows me to my office and all I see is a giant adorable teddy bear crossed with a kicked puppy dog. He's a good-looking man with a strong jawline and full lips, but his broad shoulders are hunched over and his head hangs low.

He's beaten and if he didn't have me, I have no doubt he'd roll over versus fight her.

I'm not going to let that happen.

At my door, I spin and address Paul. "Get a cease and desist order over to SMZ. Threaten them with libel and defamation suits if they release even a hint of this story without all of their facts being checked. That should buy us at least forty-eight hours."

"I'm on it." Paul turns to Aggie and offers his hand. "Don't worry Mr. Dunham. We'll clear this up and get you your life back soon."

"Thanks, Mr. Mendelssohn."

"Come on in, Aggie." I open my door and walk straight to the minibar in the corner. "Would you like something to drink?"

"No, ma'am." Aggie stands in the doorway with his hands in his jogger pockets.

"Call me Deidre." I make two Scotch and sodas, handing him one anyway. "Take a seat."

"Thanks." Aggie looks around my office at the seat availability but doesn't make a move.

I grab his hand and lead him to the couch, wanting to make this as informal as possible. He's overwhelmed, and right now I need to be his friend, even though I'd like to be more. I've had a crush on him since we drafted him three years ago, but considering he was married and I'm a Scott, that wasn't even a remote possibility.

Technically, it still isn't. Nevertheless, the impossibility of it all hasn't stopped me from fantasizing about him.

There are people in the industry that consider me a bully. My brothers lovingly call me Ball-Buster, or Buster for short. Either way, I'm definitely not someone who backs down, but if you are in my circle, I'll fight tooth and nail to defend you.

Cross one of mine and I'll destroy you with a smile on my face.

By being a Ranger, Aggie automatically gets my protection—that is, unless I thought he was guilty. I never did, but I needed that raw response he gave me a minute ago because I will use it against his accuser.

I know a lot more about his situation than he realizes. For instance, I know his soon-to-be ex-wife was having an affair last season with a third-string defensive lineman who found himself let go before game fourteen. That wasn't a coincidence. We're a family team and don't let shit like that fly within our ranks. Of course, I would never tell Aggie I know about her infidelity. I'm sure the entire situation has been humiliating for him—a teammate and his wife betraying him. Only a few teammates talked to him about it—Declan being one of them— convincing him to dump her lying, cheating ass.

Since then, I've been digging up dirt on Ellen Dunham and her clique of spouses. As it is, we have a players' wives luncheon later in the week while the guys are on the road. It should be fun, considering what I have planned for them.

They thought I was a bitch before? They have seen nothing yet.

"My understanding is Ellen is contesting the divorce." I sit at the other end of the little loveseat, our knees touching because of our long legs.

He glances down at our knees and presses his lips together, his eyes on the carpet between his splayed thighs. "Yeah. She doesn't want to give up the lifestyle.

Initially, she proclaimed her undying love, but eventually she admitted that no amount of money will make her leave me in this world without her. She feels she deserves everything I have and more considering she worked while I went to school."

"What kind of work did she do?"

"She worked at the makeup counter at a department store for four years."

Hmmm. Isn't that interesting?

"So, she thinks if she fights long enough, you'll give up?" I arch my brow and take a deep drink off my glass.

He shrugs. "Our entire life is her digging in her heels and me giving her whatever she wants."

"Why?" This defeatist attitude makes no sense to me. This is not the personality he wears on the field. Aggie is strong, indomitable, a leader on the line and well respected by his peers. I know because I watch him more than I should.

Mostly, I stay away from the players. Getting entangled with one of them is trouble I can't bring into the family, but Aggie gained my attention the day Deacon and Dad started talking about him at the dinner table, and I've had a crush on him ever since. I looked him up to make sure there was no drama—a small part of the vetting process when looking at draft picks—and his roguish good looks instantly intrigued me. Of course, he came to the team married, a rarity when we're drafting right out of college and I had to put my crush behind lock and key.

"It's just easier." He frowns. "I know, I'm pathetic."

"What do you want, Aggie? Do you want to fix your

marriage?" It kills me to ask him this, considering I've heard about how awful she is to him, but it doesn't benefit me or the team to have him pining over a woman, no matter how vile the rest of us think she is.

"No. I want nothing to do with her, although I don't want to see her hurt. All I want is to play football." He brings his soft brown eyes up to mine. "This game, being part of this team, is the only thing that makes me happy."

"It's my job to make sure nothing stops you from doing that." I pat his knee and stand up, taking his untouched whiskey and downing it in one ballsy gulp. Nothing makes me nervous and yet Aggie makes the butterflies in my belly flutter. Maybe it's because he's never flirted with me, never looked at me for more than a couple of seconds, that makes him irresistible.

Maybe it's because I see the bullied boy trapped in a man's body that brings my mama bear's instincts roaring to life. "I have something to admit, Aggie."

"Yes, ma'am?" He also stands.

"I've been investigating Ellen ever since the restraining order, and if you truly want this over, you're going to have to stop being nice and go on the offensive as only someone like me can."

He shakes his head, keeping his eyes cast low. What I wouldn't do to have his gaze on me? "I don't understand."

Declan pops his head into my office, his bright blue eyes going from me to his offensive lineman. "How's it going in here?"

"I was getting ready to lay some more heavy news on

Aggie and then tell him my plan on how we're going to fix it."

Declan smiles and smacks his palms together, rubbing them like a villain on a Saturday morning cartoon. "This ought to be good. My sister schemes like no other."

I roll my eyes. "Declan, you don't get automatic access just because you are the team captain, the quarterback, or a Scott, but I'll let you stay if Aggie wants you here."

Aggie shrugs. "Can it get any more humiliating?"

I shrug back, my heart breaking for him because yes—yes it can.

"Come on in, Declan. Grab a drink." Aggie motions to the bar with a wry chuckle. I hope by the time I'm done with Ellen he will really smile and become the man I see on the practice field. I believe him when he says all he wants to do is play football. He is truly happy when amongst his teammates.

I wish I could be part of what makes him happy, but at least I can be the one handing him his well-deserved peace.

"As I said, I've been investigating Ellen ever since she contested the divorce and you had to file a restraining order against her. My investigator reported back last week with some photos that lead us to believe your divorce lawyer is fucking you over and—" I glance at Declan and then back to Aggie who once again is inspecting the carpet "—probably fucking her, too."

He sighs. "Figures."

"I'd like you to fire him now and hire Ms. Kristi Tindleson." Grabbing a card off my desk, I hand it to him. "I've already briefed her on the details as I know them, and she will resolve your divorce quickly, quietly and thoroughly."

"She doesn't need weeks to come up to speed?" he asks, flipping the card over in his hand.

"No. She knows enough to sketch out a game plan. We think she can have you divorced within the month." I lick my lips and tilt my head to Declan, who moves Aggie over to a club chair and then sits beside him on the loveseat with a drink in his hand.

"I can't pay her upfront." Aggie glances at me before returning his eyes to the ground.

"What do you mean?"

"My accounts are frozen. I can't access my money."

Alarms sound off in my head and anger simmers in my belly. How long has he been living like this? Ten weeks I have to assume, maybe longer. "That'll be the first thing Kristi fixes. Meanwhile, I'm having forensic experts peel through these pictures to see if they can prove it is makeup versus real bruising, but having Ellen admit the truth would be the best answer and the one I'm going to work on getting from her."

He shakes his head, bringing his soft brown eyes up to meet mine. "She'll never admit she faked the photos. Ever."

"We'll see," I say with supreme confidence. "What do you say, Aggie? Can we call Myron Peterson and tell him the good news?"

"Now? Okay. Sure." He pulls his phone out and dials the number.

"Put it on speaker, if you don't mind," I say, exchanging a look with Declan, who merely smirks and shakes his head. I don't think he knew about the frozen accounts and is probably just as angry as I am, but he knows I love calling someone out on their bullshit and making them sweat with the unknown of what's coming for them. A hint of retribution that may or may not come to fruition. I'd rather leave someone battling their own demons and letting their evil deeds pick at them like a festering scab with the idea I'm waiting on the fringe, ready to do what karma isn't working fast enough to deliver.

"Mr. Dunham. How can I help you?" Myron says with a smugness that grates on me. I have dual masters degrees in communications and marketing, but I also minored in pre-law. I could have gone the contract lawyer route, but realized the family and team were better served with me recognizing that Paul Mendelssohn is best for us.

"Yeah, Mr. Peterson. I'm going to have to let you go." Aggie shakes his head and closes his eyes. He almost sounds repentant that he has to fire him, which brings my mama bear's claws out.

"You can't fire me, Aggie. Not when we are so close to finalizing the divorce."

"Actually," I walk over and practically stand over Aggie, his scented body wash hitting my nostrils just right. I'd love to close my eyes and breathe him in, but now is neither the time nor the place. "You mean he can't fire you when you're so close to helping his wife fuck him over."

"Who is this?" Myron barks instead of denying it.

"This is Deidre Scott, President of Communications for the Rangers football team, and we're fully aware of the game you've been playing the last few months. I have photographic evidence, as well as audio confirmation, of your inappropriate relationship with Ellen Dunham, and while none of that would hold up in court, I'm betting it's enough to have you disbarred. A first year law student could have kept Mr. Dunham's accounts from being frozen, or from having him removed from his home when he's not the one with a criminal record. By the time I'm done with you, I'll have your worthless law degree hanging over my desk like a big-game safari trophy."

"Uhhh..." Mr. Peterson stammers.

"The only thing to come out of your mouth right now that might grant you an ounce of clemency is a sincere heartfelt apology to Mr. Dunham. Otherwise, don't waste your breath. Good evening, Mr. Peterson."

I perch on top of my desk and cross my long legs, tapping the speaker on my phone. It rings once before my friend Kristi Tindleson answers.

"Hey."

"Hi. I have Mr. Dunham here, and he's ready to begin."

"Great. Hi, Aggie. Can I call you Aggie?" she says sweetly. The thing about Kristi is that she's just as cutthroat as I am, only she hides it behind cashmere sweaters with pearl buttons. In some ways, she's even more bloodthirsty than me and I love her for it.

He stands up and slides his phone back into his pocket. I'm not sure if he hung up on Mr. Peterson, and honestly I don't care. Let that shitbag know he's being replaced by the best divorce attorney in Colorado. He'll piss himself. "Aggie is fine, ma'am."

"Great. Let's meet in the morning. My office? 9am?"

"Yes, ma'am." He nods, his hands once again in his pockets, but now he's holding his head up, his beautiful eyes with their long delicate eyelashes on me, a faint smile on his lips.

"I'll call you later, chick." I smile back at him, my eyes locked on his for the moment, and hit the speaker to end the call.

For what feels like an eternity, we stare into each other's eyes. Gratitude paints his features, a weight lifting from his shoulders as his chest expands, and he takes a full cleansing breath. I want nothing more than to stand up and wrap my arms around him, pull his face into my neck and whisper into his ear how it'll all be over soon and I'll be waiting for him on the other side of this.

Of course, I can't do that.

We must stare at each other longer than appropriate because Declan stands and clears his throat. "Is that it for tonight? Can we go eat now? I'm starving and I'm sure Aggie is, too."

For the first time in my life, I break eye contact first, a slight blush hitting my cheeks. "Yeah, I think that will be it for tonight. Keep doing what you've been doing, Aggie.

Don't answer your phone and don't accept a visit from her. I suspect she'll go batshit crazy as soon as Mr. Peterson informs her of the change. Meanwhile, if you can stop by my office before practice tomorrow, that would be good."

"We don't have practice tomorrow, Buster." Declan shakes his head.

That's right... the day after a game they rest. "I forgot."

"Lunch?" Aggie offers. "I finally have an appetite."

I flash him a sweet smile, thrilled to have him suggest something as intimate as a meal together. "I'll text you my number tonight and we can go from there."

"Sounds good," Aggie pauses and then rolls his neck, his eyes sparkling as he flashes me a genuine smile. "Deidre."

I watch him follow my brother out of my office, my heart skipping a beat. A glimmer of hope—the one I'm providing him—made that man transform before my eyes.

I can't wait to see who he becomes over the next couple of weeks.

Chapter Three
Aggie

Declan drives me back to Devlin's house. I'd already called to let him know what craziness might come, and he, in turn, informed security. Even though he should be out with the guys tonight, he opted to stay and hang out with me and the star quarterback as we feast and watch movies.

My teammates are good friends. They are my only friends. Ellen cut me off from everyone else over the years, including my family. I can't believe I didn't initiate this divorce a long time ago.

I really am a sucker.

"Your sister..." I trail off, because what else can I say? I can't tell Declan I've always had an inappropriate infatuation with her, one I would never have acted on while married, but one that I will now fantasize about as the upcoming weeks look brighter than ever for me.

Declan chuckles. "She's something else, huh?"

"Do you think she can really make Ellen give up and go away?"

"Yeah, man. She'll make Ellen wish she'd never met you." Declan nods to the security guard who bends down to see me crammed into the passenger seat of his BMW 8-Series. He's around six-foot five and had the car modified to move the seats back an additional six inches, and I still have my knees against the dash.

"Mr. Dunham. Mr. Frank has alerted us to the potential activity this evening, and we've got you covered."

"Sorry for the inconvenience, but it might be crazy for the next couple weeks."

"That's what we are here for, sir."

"And I thank God for you."

Declan fist bumps the security guard and then drives through the gate, leaving them behind.

I sigh. "I'm going to have to buy those guys cars or something by the time this is over."

"Why didn't you tell me she had your accounts frozen?" Declan frowns and shakes his head. "What have you been living on for the last however many weeks?"

"Devlin." I lower my head. "He feeds and shelters me. He offered to buy me clothes, but that's where I drew the line. I'll never be able to repay him for his friendship as it is."

"He's a good guy, but you have a team full of friends." Declan pulls into Devlin's driveway and parks in front of the garage. "I know this situation sucks and is embarrassing—"

"Humiliating. Utterly and emphatically humiliating," I correct him.

He sighs. "You aren't the first guy to be made a sucker of by a woman. Hell, at least you were married to yours. How many hot groupies or bendy girlfriends have taken the guys for a ride?"

"I'd rather be hustled out of a hundred grand worth of clothing or a car than cheated on with one of my teammates. That's betrayal times two." I pop the door open and unfold myself from the passenger seat.

"True. But he was a dickhead and a shitty defensive linebacker, so I'd hardly call him a teammate. We were looking for a reason to let him go, anyway."

His comment makes me stop. "Wait. What? I thought they let him go because he was at the end of his contract?"

Declan's expression contorts, and he slides his hand down his face. "Uh, yeah, that's what we told the public. The truth is, as soon as I heard the rumor, I went to the family and the decision was made. We can't have that kind of drama in the team, so he had to go."

"You picked me over him?"

"Dude. It wasn't even a choice. Of course, we picked you. I couldn't do what I do without you." Declan smacks me on the back as we walk up the path to the front door where Devlin stands in matching jogger pants and a loose hoodie.

Frick and Frack here. "Look at the three of us living the dream."

"We're on lock down anyway, so what's it matter?" Devlin laughs and hands me a pizza box.

"We're on lock down?" I glance at Declan, who shrugs.

"The GM wants us to chill out for a couple of weeks. Too much bad press lately with the strip club brawl a couple weeks ago and the DUI last week. He wants nothing overshadowing our championship season."

"Dang. The team has to hate me right now."

Devlin shakes his head. "They don't know what's going on. Hell, I don't know what's going on."

"And they won't know as long as Deidre can keep it out of the media. Only if it hits the front page will we brief the team about the specifics. Right now, all they know is to stay away from Ellen, keep their wives away from Ellen, and to keep their mouths shut with a canned *no comment* if asked about you or the divorce."

We walk into the kitchen where Devlin has a smorgasbord to choose from. My stomach rumbles, although the high I felt walking out of Deidre's office has subsided with this news. My personal drama shouldn't affect my teammates.

Devlin pops open a seltzer water and hands it to me, knowing I don't drink often. "You don't have to tell me, but what is going on?"

I shove a slice of pizza into my mouth and chew while shaking my head. "She claimed I beat and raped her two nights ago, sending pictures of her battered face to SMZ."

Devlin casts a set of wide eyes at me and then Declan. "Fucking bitch."

"That's what I said." Declan nods.

"No police report? Just straight to SMZ, huh?" Devlin shakes his head.

"Can't go to the police or the hospital if it never happened," Declan points out.

"True. Jesus. You okay, man?" Devlin leans his ass against the counter and crosses his arms over his chest.

"Yeah. No." I shake my head. "I don't know."

"It's going to be fine." Declan flips open a couple of to-go containers before helping himself to a plate of nachos. "Deidre will have this settled by the time we get back from Florida, and you'll be divorced this time next month."

Devlin cracks open another seltzer water and hands it to Declan and then lifts his own can. "Here's to getting this shit handled and moving on with your life as a sexy, bad ass, offensive lineman from the national championship football team. Let's go Rangers!"

I chuckle and clink my can with them, but in the back of my mind I keep thinking about my lunch date with Deidre tomorrow. I can't believe I asked her out—in a roundabout way. The words slipped out of my mouth before I could stop them and, thankfully, she jumped on them with veiled enthusiasm, as if lunch with me wouldn't be so bad.

What will it be like, and where will we go?

What will we talk about when we aren't talking about my screwed up life and Ellen?

Crap, I guess I should have let Devlin take me clothes shopping for at least one nice outfit. What am I going to wear tomorrow?

Deidre is smart and beautiful, educated and sophisticated, while I'm a big, clumsy guy who grew up in a trailer set on a dried-up piece of land along I-10 in central Texas. Sure, I have a business degree, but let's be honest about how much education I actually have—which is little to none. I don't have a clue what I'm going to do when I can't play football. I've never thought beyond possibly coaching, and even that is a dream I'm not sure how to fulfill.

And then my phone beeps in my pocket. I pull it out to see a text message.

> This is Deidre. Send me a note tomorrow when you're wrapping up your meeting with Kristi. I suspect it will be close to lunchtime when you're done.

My heart thumps in my chest—a teenage excitement foreign to my six-foot seven, two hundred and eight-five-pound body radiates through my limbs. This is the first text message I've ever exchanged with a woman beyond Ellen.

Seriously.

She wouldn't let me have any female friends or business associates. One time, they paired me up with a female classmate for a project in my college economics class, and Ellen lost her ever-loving mind, making our lives a living hell until the project was over.

To think, there was a time she'd convinced me that was what love looks like.

"I will. Thank you for everything you've done for me."

Her response is immediate.

"I have done nothing yet, Aggie, but you're welcome. You deserve to be happy and I'm going to help you get there."

I smile to myself. Sappy responses about how she could make me happy flit through my mind, but that is dumb and cheesy and super inappropriate.

Declan arches his brow. "Is that my sister?"

"Yeah." I slide my phone back into my pocket. "We're meeting for lunch tomorrow after my meeting with the divorce attorney."

He nods, but his eyes are on me as if he's trying to peer into my brain and decipher all my thoughts. That I cannot have. I'll share everything with him but my private thoughts about his sister. Those are for me and me alone.

After a good night's sleep, and a fantastic meeting with Ms. Tindleson—who already filed paperwork to have my assets unfrozen and Ellen's name removed from my accounts—I'm feeling pretty confident about the divorce proceedings. She's scheduled a hearing three weeks from today in front of a judge, something that seems miraculous considering Mr. Peterson said we couldn't get a court date for at least another two months.

I guess now I know he was lying about everything.

Walking out of her office, I pull out my phone and send a quick text to Deidre.

> Where would you like to eat? Can I come pick you up at the office?

> Actually, I'm at my place north of Starlite Park. Would you mind coming up here? I had lunch catered in.

My heart thumps against my rib cage and something drops like a lead weight in my belly. Lunch with Deidre Scott at her home?

Alone?

No way.

I text back with a casualness I do not feel.

> Not a problem. Send me the address and I'll head that way. Do you want me to pick something up?

> 16453 Scott Drive. No, I have everything. See you soon.

I punch her address into my maps app and follow the roads north of town until I pass large houses on acres of land. The farther north I drive, the larger and more secluded the houses get until all I pass are gated drive-ways through heavy trees without a house in sight. I knew the Scotts were wealthy, but this is beyond my wildest imagination.

Is this where Declan grew up? Dang.

I get to an entrance with stone and wrought-iron gates thrown open. Tentatively, I maneuver Devlin's custom Bronco up the concrete driveway to a beautiful house styled like a Mediterranean villa. My house south of here isn't shabby. At eleven million a year, Ellen made sure we bought a big, expensive house fitting our new status, but it is nothing compared to this.

Deidre walks out the front door wearing an emerald green halter dress with a flowing skirt that swings in the gentle breeze, her shoulders bare and kissed by the sun. Jeez, she is breathtaking, and I can't help but stare at her dumbly as she waves from the porch.

Imagine coming home to her every day?

Wearing khakis and a white button-down shirt—the nicest clothes I let Devlin buy me—I'm kicking myself for not stopping and buying her a bouquet.

Although, this isn't a date, so why would my cheesy ass bring her flowers?

Think, Aggie. Think.

Don't make a fool of yourself in front of Ms. Scott, the only daughter of your boss and a woman completely out of your league. Besides, I'm here to get help with Ellen, not romance the most beautiful woman I've ever met.

"Did you have a hard time finding my house?" She smiles as I approach her on the front steps.

"Not at all. This is really something."

She shrugs, looking a little sheepish. "It's on the backside of my parent's property. They gifted me twenty acres of their land and told me to build a house. It's obnoxious, I know."

"Your parents and grandparents worked hard to give you the best, and now you work hard to help the family keep that legacy. There's nothing wrong with that, and you should be proud of what you have—gifted and earned."

She stares at me for a second, surprised by my words, and motions to the front door. "Come on in. Are you hungry?"

"Look at me." I pat my thick belly. "I'm starved."

"You're a big man who burns big calories, so you should have a big appetite." She throws me a wink and leads me into her house.

Dear God. Is Deidre Scott flirting with me?

No. That's not possible.

I follow her into a tastefully decorated living space that feels posh but welcoming. Like, I could imagine relaxing on these couches, not bypassing them because *they are only for guests*. On a large quartz countertop is a couple of trays of BBQ, judging by the mouthwatering aroma.

"Would you like to eat in the kitchen, dining room, or on the terrace?" she asks.

"You tell me. I'm easy."

She grins and hands me a plate. "Let's eat on the terrace. It's too beautiful of a day to waste. What can I get you to drink?"

"Water works for me." I look into the trays, peeling back the silver domes like at a fancy buffet, to find roasted chicken thighs, brisket, potatoes, corn and salad. "This is one heck of a feast."

"I grew up with two professional football player brothers. I know what it takes to keep you well fed." She grabs a bottle of Perrier and two glasses. "Can I ask you a question?"

"Sure."

"Do you never drink, or are you not drinking with me?"

Chapter Four
Deidre

Aggie's cheeks turn a bright pink as he shrugs. "I'm not a big drinker, and I refrain during the season."

"Interesting. My brother has the same ritual the night before a game. It's almost like a superstition."

"Well, we want to be at our best on game day."

"No other reason?" I throw him an arched eyebrow when he looks up at me.

He sighs. "Ellen's the drinker, so I learned early on that one of us had to have a clear head."

Reaching out, I wrap my fingers around his forearm and give him a gentle squeeze. "Understood."

We fill our plates and make our way out to the terrace. "So, Aggie, I hope you don't mind me asking, but how was your meeting with Kristi?"

He smiles and I see his body morph, visibly relaxing as he settles into his chair. "She's amazing. For the first time in a long time, I feel hopeful about my future outside of football."

"Good." I dig into my food with gusto because, for one, I'm starving, and two, I want Aggie to feel comfortable in front of me. Something tells me he's used to being criticized and therefore probably overthinks every little expression crossing my face. My heart breaks to think he has been treated like anything other than the wonderful man I believe him to be.

He smiles, watching as I take a couple big bites of brisket. "I've never seen a woman like you eat actual food."

"What's that supposed to mean?"

Shrugging, he casts his eyes down at his plate. "You're tall, thin and statuesque. Absolutely gorgeous—" he murmurs those two words "—so I assume you drink green smoothies and eat kale salads."

I choose not to react to the words that may or may not have been meant for my ears, but inside I'm giddy.

He thinks I'm gorgeous.

"Absolutely not. I had two brothers to compete with growing up, and I can out-eat both of them."

"I refuse to believe that." He chuckles.

His smile, the sound of his laugh, does something to my heart. I wouldn't consider myself the type of woman drawn to guys who need to be saved, but considering the men I'm surrounded by—pure testosterone and unshakeable confidence—maybe I've never met a man like Aggie before. "I guess I'll have to invite you to a family dinner one night."

He blushes again and changes the subject. "This is fantastic BBQ."

I let him get a few more bites in before I lean back in my chair and cross my legs. "The reason I wanted to meet with you after your appointment with Kristi is because your situation isn't going to get better just by having the best divorce attorney in the state representing you."

"It's not?"

"No, Aggie. You can tell me I'm wrong, but I don't think a clear-cut divorce, restraining order, or judge's orders are going to stop Ellen from coming after you. The photos she sent to SMZ are proof of that, don't you think?"

"That's true." He pushes back from the table and leans forward so his elbows are resting on his knees, making his massive biceps bulge against the taut fabric of his cotton button-down shirt.

I try not to be distracted by his well-formed torso and get down to brass tacks. "My plan with all adversaries is basically the same. First, I call a meeting where I lay out the facts as I know them and then explain how whatever they want isn't going to happen. Then, I usually play the pseudo-nice guy card and present them with an alternate, albeit less attractive option to consider. This is where I need to understand what it is you want regarding Ellen and your future."

"For example?"

"For example—she's living in your house while you're sleeping in Devlin's basement. I'm not exactly sure how that happened, but what is it you want? Do you want your house back?"

"No, that house was never me, and I can't see

myself living in it after this is said and done. However, if I could have my dream of dreams, we'd sell the house, and I'd give her the money she needs to buy her own place—" he chuckles "—preferably in College Station, Texas."

I smile. "That was going to be my second question. Obviously, I feel she is toxic and dangerous to the team. Not only because of her interaction with the other players' wives, but her desire to humiliate you publicly, so I'd like to see her leave Colorado, but I wasn't sure how you felt about that."

"I think she was happiest in Texas when we were living in a bigger city where she was working and had friends and coworkers, although I doubt that's what she would say."

"So, as part of your divorce agreement, you're willing to sell the house and split the profits so she can buy her own place?"

"Yes. That's what Ms. Tindleson and I discussed this morning. Ellen's already burned all my clothes, but I would like my dog, truck and the guns my daddy gave me before we had our falling out." Aggie presses his lips together and looks over the balcony of my terrace to the acres of trees beyond, a small dimple forming in his right cheek as his brow furrows with what I can only assume is regret.

"You had a falling out with your family?"

"Kind of. Ellen had a falling out with my family, and she made keeping in touch with them difficult. I haven't talked to my parents in years."

"I'm so sorry to hear that. Does that mean your parents have never seen you play a professional game?"

He shakes his head. "They never even got to see me play college ball."

"They didn't come to your graduation?" My jaw drops slightly.

"Ellen refused to invite them."

My head is spinning. I don't understand how he could've allowed her to isolate him like she did. Being together since elementary school is the only thing that makes sense, because I think if Aggie had ever gotten a taste of independence or freedom, he would've never put up with the way she treated him.

"Do you think you'll reach out to your family once the divorce is final?"

"It's something I think about a lot, but I'm not sure how that conversation would go."

Oh my God. I want nothing more than to crawl into his lap and throw my arms around his neck and simply hold him. How lonely has his life been while married to her?

My own dating history is nothing to be proud of. I've dated my fair share of losers. Coming from a wealthy family like mine seems to attract guys with beautiful smiles, flashy cars and empty hearts. I don't think one boyfriend was faithful to me, and I doubt one marriage proposal was sincere. They all fell hard and fast—some love-bombing me, some gaslighting me—but with brothers like mine, none of them got very far. Even Declan, as my younger sibling, was critical of the men

I've brought home. Maybe if Aggie had siblings like mine, Ellen would never have gotten her talons into him.

He brings his eyes to mine. "You're not going to hurt her, are you?"

I chuckle. "Describe hurt?"

"I want this over. I want to restart my personal life. And although I have every reason to hate her, I can't bring myself to do it. I wish her all the happiness in the world, as long as it is far away from me."

I take a deep breath and let it out slowly before rising to my feet and grabbing our plates. "You're a good man, Aggie. I can't promise you her feelings won't get hurt. She's not going to like being told no, and I doubt she'll like the options I present her either."

Aggie also stands, taking the plates from me. His eyes search my face, but what he's looking for is unclear. "Do you do this for all the players with messy divorces?"

I suck my breath in, because I now understand what he's trying to mete out. "Are you asking me if you're special?"

He blushes but does not respond.

"Ellen is threatening not only your reputation, but the team's reputation, something no other player's personal life has done to date."

Pressing his lips together, he nods. "Understood."

I wrap my fingers around his powerful forearm to stop him, a litany of confessions dancing on the tip of my tongue, but I swallow them down. "You are special—to me."

I t's been four days since our lunch and it's taken everything within me not to text Aggie. A relationship with him is impossible. Not only because he's one of our players, but because he's still legally married and I'm handling aspects of his divorce. The more information my investigator digs up, the more I hate but also pity Ellen. She's losing an amazing man, and while she might have known it at one time, she ruined any chance at a happily-ever-after with him years ago by the things she has done.

I wonder if once she started down this path she couldn't stop herself, even though she knew it was wrong? She's been lying to him for years about all kinds of things, including a separate bank account where she's been stockpiling cash. Six point four million to be exact—all in her name—as well as an ocean-front house on Myrtle Beach and a condo in College Station, Texas, totaling another one point seven million in assets.

When did she have time to acquire these properties, you might ask? She signed both deeds while the team was traveling for an away game.

Ellen is smarter and craftier than I was expecting, and the agent she had helping her does most of his business through the Peterson Law Group, which tells me she's been fucking him for a long time and somehow steered Aggie into hiring him as his lawyer.

I wonder how she did that?

My source at SMZ says I scare his editor enough to stall the story, but also that Ellen has been feeding him drool worthy headline fodder the last few days, and that has him weighing the pros and cons of going up against me—which means I need to act soon.

But first, the players' wives' luncheon this afternoon, where I toe the line of *we're one big happy family* and *I will crush you if you damage the reputation of this organization.* As my mother repeatedly reminds me, it's not appropriate to dictate how people conduct their private lives. Honestly, I agree—especially as I fantasize about an impossible future with Aggie—but in the end, it is my job to ensure the team is protected. Luckily, I've only identified two wives as potential troublemakers in the absence of Ellen. Hopefully, their marriages are more important than any *let's be famous* ideas she's put into their heads.

My mother, Linda Scott, will lead the luncheon with London and me at her side.

That's right. This is London's first family event as the future Mrs. Deacon Scott. This luncheon is part of the players' wives' auxiliary committee where we give back to the community through the players' various charities. We'll chat and discuss which charity events we want to schedule over the next couple of months leading into the holidays, and at some point I'll softly drop my hammer. Softly... my mother reiterated for the hundredth time thirty minutes ago.

If I'm lucky, the players already brought the message

home Sunday night and everything I say will be a gentle reminder.

Fucking hell... nothing about me is gentle, especially when I open my mouth.

My phone beeps.

> Happy Friday. I hope reaching out is okay. There are rumors that Ellen might try to crash the luncheon the players' wives are having. I wanted to give you a heads up.

> You can reach out to me anytime about anything. I hope you consider me a friend, as well as an ally. Security is on alert as we have banned her from all Rangers activities. She couldn't even enter the stadium with a paid ticket at this point.

After a few minutes of him not responding, I send another text.

> Are you on your way to the airport?

I know the team takes off in the next hour as my father and brothers were leaving the house around the same time as my mother and I.

> Yeah, we're driving now.

> Have a great flight. Don't do anything I wouldn't do tonight. 😉

Oh my God, I suck at casual flirting. Direct and to the point is more my speed.

> One, we're on lock down. Two, I'm not the partying type. And three, I don't know what you wouldn't do.

I bite my lip to suppress my smile. This is the kind of flirting I can do. It takes all my willpower not to feed right into it, turning what might be an innocuous comment from him into something masturbation worthy for both of us later.

> That's a discussion for another time, if you really want to know.

> Another time then.

Wow. How do I respond to that?

Chapter Five
Aggie

I walk out of the courtroom somber, yet relieved. Ever since Ms. Tindleson took my case, my life has changed. I no longer have a sense of impending doom hanging over my head. The bands wrapped around my chest have loosened, and I finally feel like I can take full, deep breaths.

I feel like I did on draft night—like my entire world is about to change, the next phase even more epic than the last.

My cell phone, the electronic accessory I once felt shackled by, has been silent for almost four weeks. It's almost like Ellen lost my number. She hasn't pulled one antic since I fired Mr. Peterson, adhering to the restraining order she previously ignored.

Today, I got what I wanted—a divorce and ultimately, freedom.

Ellen got more than enough to start over with no reason to come back to me for anything. I gave her everything appropriate to Colorado law despite my lawyer's advice to leave her with nothing. I never wanted to screw Ellen over, I only wanted her to move on and leave me in peace. Of course, she was pissed when my lawyer revealed her hidden assets—a secret bank account and two properties—and listed them as part of the estate to be divided, but she tamped down her outrage in front of the judge. In the end, he granted her fifty percent of all that we acquired during our time together, as I expected. She has until next Friday to move out of the house, and we'll list it on the market the following week. Once it's sold, we'll split the profits and that will truly be the end of us.

Oh... I asked for one thing. I requested she legally change back to her maiden name.

She agreed, for one hundred grand.

Done. I would've paid more to sever my name from her future shenanigans, which I'm sure are coming.

I walk to my truck, the one Ms. Tindleson gained the keys for three weeks ago, my phone beeping in my pocket at the same time Ellen approaches me in the parking lot.

"You got what you want." She crosses her arms over her chest and stares up at me with the puppy dog eyes that used to break me.

Not wanting to fight with her, I glance around to make sure we have some kind of audience—just in case she swings at me again. "The restraining order is still in effect, Ellen. You can't be here right now."

She shakes her head, a rogue tear falling down her cheeks. If it's real, I don't know—nor do I care. Not anymore. "We've known each other since we were eight years old. You really have no intention of talking to me ever again?"

I sigh and clasp my hands in front of me. "We've said everything that needs to be said over the last six months. It's over now. Enjoy your life. I hope you can find the happiness you're looking for." Unlocking my truck door, I hop in without giving her a second glance. I can't engage her because I know what she's capable of. Eventually, she'll work herself up into a screaming, fist-throwing tantrum, and I can't have that. Part of me wonders if she's on some kind of medication to mellow her out, because I've honestly never seen her this calm or in control. I really hope she gets the help she needs to have a happy life—one that does not include me.

Thankfully, she turns and walks away without incident. I'm pulling out of the parking lot when I remember my phone beeping with a message.

Checking my text, I'm thrilled and surprised to see one from Deidre. We haven't exchanged a word since that one text nearly a month ago.

Is it crazy that I miss her?

> I believe your court hearing was this morning, unless something changed. How are you holding up?

> Can you talk? I'm driving.

I dictate back, putting my phone in the dash cradle.

Seconds later, my phone rings and Deidre's beautiful husky voice fills the cab of my truck. "Hi."

"Ms. Scott. How are you?"

"Are we back to Ms. Scott?"

"Well, it has been a while since we talked." I chuckle, the first genuine smile of the day spreading my lips.

"Yeah, I know. I didn't think it was appropriate to have casual conversations with you while you were prepping for your divorce. How did it go today?"

I hear her clicking on her computer, so I'm guessing she's sitting at her desk with me on speaker.

"We just finished. It went fine. Perfect, actually. No drama at all."

"That's great, Aggie. How are you feeling?" I can feel her smile through the audio, her genuine happiness infusing me with warmth.

"Relieved." I shrug to no one. "A little overwhelmed at everything I need to do."

"Like what?" Her fingers stop clacking against her keyboard.

"Well, Declan gave me his realtor, but I'm not sure I want to buy right now. I think the smart move would be to rent for a little while until we see what happens with the team."

"What are you talking about?" Her voice pitches a little, surprise lacing her tone.

"I'm approaching the end of my three-year contract. There's no guarantee about where I'll be next year."

"Are you thinking about leaving?" She curses under her breath. "I'm sorry. This is not a conversation I should have with you. Contract negotiations are none of my business until it's time to announce them."

"Are we talking as friends or as employer slash employee?"

"Shit." She curses again. "I've never had to differentiate between the two before except with my brothers and that's different."

I take in a deep breath and let it out slowly. "Well, if I was talking to my friend, I would say I'm not looking to leave. I love this team and the area, but the organization has to do what is best for the team and I understand that."

She's quiet for a moment. "As a friend, I would say, based upon your on-field performance and the quarterback's love for you, you have a long future with the Rangers—if you want it."

Smiling, I take a left into Devlin's neighborhood. Per the judge, I have time scheduled for this Wednesday with a sheriff's escort to visit the house and collect the last of my things. I don't care about the furniture, kitchenware, art, knick knacks, etc. She can take them or sell them for all I care. If there is anything left of my clothes or my guns, I'll grab those, as well as any paperwork. Thankfully, I got my dog in the divorce and Devlin is fine with letting Rev stay with us at the house until I get my own place. I don't think he's much of a dog person, but Rev is a well-trained Cockapoo and shouldn't be a nuisance.

Yes, I have a twenty-pound lap dog versus some gigantic attack animal. He's my snuggle buddy above all else, and I've missed him more than anything.

Crap—I'm going to have to look into a quality dog sitter this week for our next away game.

"I suppose you and the guys will celebrate tonight," Deidre says barely above a whisper.

"We're still on lockdown, remember?"

"I think management will lift that soon. You should go out and have a good time. You deserve it. Let the guys take you to a strip club or something."

I snort. "Why is everyone pushing me to go to the strip club?"

"I don't know. I thought it was the thing to do."

"For some guys. Others like to go to dance clubs. Neither of those interest me."

"You don't enjoy having near naked women dance for you?" she says with a joking lilt to her tone. I think she's teasing me, but without seeing her face, I can't be sure.

I pull into the garage and kill the engine, closing my eyes to envision what Deidre would look like dancing on stage. She certainly has the body for it, but does she have the moves? I bet she does. She carries herself with the confidence of a woman who knows how to move her body, but I can't imagine she would ever perform for an audience of more than one. Call it pedigree, refined class, or discriminating taste, but I don't see Deidre jumping up on a table at a party so that all eyes end up on her. While not shy, her commanding presence isn't based upon getting men to think with their junk. She's beautiful—she knows it—but she's also intelligent, and I suspect any man who tries to diminish her contribution to merely her sex would offend her. "I'm a simple man but smart enough to know they aren't dancing for me. Besides, I prefer stolen moments and private shows in the bedroom."

"I don't think you're simple, Aggie, but more mature than most of your teammates. Certainly more mature than your quarterback." She giggles.

"Ah, you're just saying that because he's your brother." I chuckle and enter an empty house. I guess Devlin is at the gym or maybe his new girlfriend's house.

"No, I'm saying that because I've been managing Declan's PR for the last eight years of his life and he's practically a full-time job." Deidre covers the phone and talks to someone in her office. "I've got to go. I'm glad today was successful. If you need anything, I'm only a phone call away."

"Actually..." I can't believe I'm going here, but I'm desperate to see her again—even if there can be nothing between us—and I have no idea how to spend time with her without asking her out. "I was wondering—"

"Yes?" She practically purrs, or maybe that's my imagination.

"I need to buy clothes. Specifically suits, and I suck at coordinating shirts and ties and stuff. I know a lot of guys use a stylist, but I was wondering if you'd like to go with me?"

I'm met with silence and for a few seconds I feel like the biggest fool. What am I thinking, asking the President of Communications if she wants to go shopping with me?

"I'd love to. When?"

"Uh, soon?" Holy crap, I wasn't expecting her to say yes.

"How about I text you a couple of my available dates and times, and you pick which one works for you?"

"Yeah. That sounds like a good plan."

She sighs. "I'm sorry, but I really have to go. Have fun today and don't do anything I wouldn't do."

I chuckle. "I still don't know what you wouldn't do."

"Hmmm. That's still a conversation for another time."

"I look forward to it, Deidre."

"Me too, Aggie."

Chapter Six
Deidre

I've never crushed on someone I knew I had to stay away from, which I think makes me want Aggie all the more. Is it the cliché of wanting what you can't have that makes him so damn irresistible? Or is it the shy, quiet reserve with which he interacts with me—asking, but not actually asking me out?

Lunch? Innocuous enough and yet, one hundred percent his idea.

Shopping? Again, innocent and yet, we're spending time together—getting to know each other. Something I don't do with any of the other players.

If you think about it, he's pretty smooth.

I suppose there is the possibility he's reaching out because he's lonely and in need of a friend—which I'm willing to be—but the way he steals glances at me when he thinks no one is looking makes the butterflies in my belly dance and my naughty fantasies take flight at night.

Despite my work and family obligations, which

include charitable events and social outings, I'm also lonely. It's been two years since my last boyfriend and over a year since my last conjugal visit with a *friend*. At some point in the last twelve months, I decided playing with my heart, which—no matter how hard I fight seems to be tethered to my vagina—is a bad idea. As a strong, powerful, educated boss babe, I've spent years believing I could detach emotion from sex like a man. I mean, I'm confident I can go toe to toe with any man in my field, but as I approached my thirtieth birthday, I realized the only satisfying sex I had was when I cared about the man and dreamed of a future. Then I gave myself a break from men and meaningless trysts.

Maybe I've been so desperate to meet a truly nice guy, my soul recognized him in Aggie the day we met and I've only been biding my time until he was available.

I don't know what the right answer is. I only know how I feel about him, even though I also know I have no right to feel any way about him.

My phone beeps with an incoming text.

We're done with practice. What time would you like to meet and where?

Come on up when you're ready. We can leave from here.

Is that okay?

No one's here. They've already gone home for the day.

I know he's worried about running into my father or

Deacon, both of whom would have something to say—
only they'd be talking to me, not him.

I'm the one in the Rangers' management position,
even though I have nothing to do with player retention or
their contracts.

I'm the older one of the two of us—by almost six
years.

I'm the one tempting a public scandal if our casual
flirting turns into anything more.

But is there really anything wrong with casual flirting? It's an ego boost for both of us. It makes him smile—
he certainly makes me smile—which boosts our serotonin
and dopamine levels. We just have to keep it casual and
friendly. It should be easy enough. I'll ignore the tingles
below my waist until I get to the privacy of my bedroom.
My silly crush will continue to be me and my vibrator's
secret.

"Hi." Aggie stands at my door with one hand in his
jeans pocket, the other rubbing the back of his neck.

"Hi yourself." I stand and smile, logging out of my
computer.

"Busy day today?" He smiles as he drops his head and
runs his fingers through his hair. It's been over a month
since I last saw him, and he looks like he's due for a haircut. Actually, now that I think about it, he's been growing
his hair out all season, but now it's long enough to curl
around his ears. My fingers itch to run through those
golden waves.

"Other than diffusing another gentleman's club incident from last weekend and fielding a couple of interview

requests for Devlin Frank and Declan, nothing too crazy. Are you growing your hair out?"

"I'm thinking about it. What do you think?"

"Well—" I grab my purse and round the desk to approach him "—you wear a helmet half the time, so I think growing your hair out during the season is a good idea. Have you ever had it long before?"

"No, but I've always wanted to."

I can't stop myself and reach up to run my finger through the thick hair above his ear. His hair is slightly damp, but otherwise soft and silky. "Then you should try it. It's only hair and from what I can tell, it'll look good on you."

Aggie's broad chest moves up and down with labored breaths as he stares back at me, his expression awash with something akin to need. Raw, rough edges sharpen his barely whispered words as he takes a small step back from me.

"Are we driving together or—" his words trail off.

I press my lips together, willing away my disappointment. Simple fact is, he might want me, but he'll never make a move.

Am I willing to risk being rejected and make that move? Should I?

No. Not because I can't handle the rejection, but because that's the one area of my life where I don't want to be in charge. I don't want to be the instigator, the aggressor, the ball buster. Especially not with somebody like Aggie who has spent his life being led and managed by a woman content with running all over him. I'll be attentive and receptive to any flirting he throws my way, but in the end, he has to be the one to make the first move if there's going to be anything between us. I can already feel my frustration being picked at like a raw, festering scab. And yet, I hope for the best.

"Any shop worth going to is on the north end, like our houses, so it makes little sense to drive together. Did you make an appointment with one of our tailors?"

"No. I've never actually used one of them before."

I look him up and down, the quizzical expression on my face making him chuckle. "How have you gotten away without using a tailor? There is nothing you've worn since you got out of college that could have been bought off of a rack."

"I've always gone to the big and tall shop and had them fit me there."

Shaking my head, I slip my hand into his arm—the one not offered to me—and we walk side-by-side to the elevator leading down into the garage. "I'm going to introduce you to the family tailor and we'll go from there."

We park next to each other and walk into Salvatori's. I called on our way over to make sure Gio could fit us in. Because he works on many of our football players, he carries mostly extended sizes in his store and can do everything he needs to do in the back.

"Benvenuti," Gio calls from the back as a bell rings

overhead, his daughter Celia waving from the counter with the phone pressed to her ear.

"It's us," I yell back.

"Bellissima!" A man my family knows well waltzes out from the back. He's all of five-foot nine and has been flirting with me since I was seventeen years old. For years, he joked about setting me up with his son to give him beautiful grandchildren, but I know he flirts with everybody.

"Gio. This is Aggie, one of our star offensive linemen. He needs a couple of power suits."

"Yes, of course." Gio shakes Aggie's hand. "What cut of suit do you prefer?"

Aggie's cheeks turn red. "Cut?"

Gio offers him a gentle smile. "For a man your size, I would suggest an American cut, single-breasted, solid color."

"You can't go wrong with a charcoal gray suit," I say as I thumb through a rack of jackets.

"That and perhaps a dark navy would compliment your complexion," Gio adds.

"How about a smoky gray-brown color like this?" I hold up a sleeve for Aggie and Gio's perusal.

"Oh yes. That would be a splendid color for your eyes."

Aggie shrugs. "Okay."

"How many suits do you want, sir?"

Aggie glances at me, and I lift three fingers. "At least."

"The lady says three."

"Excellent. If you follow me to the dressing room, I can get your measurements."

I watch as Aggie follows Gio, smiling as he looks back over his shoulder and winks before stepping through the heavy curtains.

Fifteen minutes later, he comes out, tucking his shirt into his pants. "That was the most thorough measure-ment taking session I've ever had."

"They do it right here. You're going to look amazing."

He blushes with the compliment. "Gio said I should pick out shirts and ties." Aggie grabs a lavender shirt with a multi-hued purple tie. "What do you think?"

"Very nice." I hold the sleeve up to his neck, letting my fingers graze his smooth jawline.

His pupils dilate and he licks his lips as he stares down at me. We hold our gaze long enough to make heat bloom in my chest, but once again, instead of acting on his feelings, Aggie takes a step back. "How about this silver-blue shirt for the dark navy suit?"

I sigh. "You seem to have a good grasp of coordinating colors. I don't think you need me here."

He grabs a mustard colored shirt and a green tie. "Really? Because I was thinking about these for the brown suit."

I chuckle and shake my head. "That's a horrible combination."

"See? I told you I need you."

"It's nice to be needed."

"Is it?" He quirks an eyebrow.

"Sometimes." I shrug.

"But would you rather be needed or wanted?"

His question surprises me.

"Both, but only for the right reasons."

"What are the wrong reasons?"

"My last name, for one."

His brow furrows as he thinks about that. "Can I ask you a personal question, Deidre?"

"Of course." I take a seat in one of the guest chairs, crossing my long legs. His eyes drop for only a second, but it's long enough for me to notice.

He towers above me, but slides his hands in his pockets and rolls his shoulders forward, as if to make himself smaller. "Why don't you have a boyfriend? You are the most beautiful woman I've ever met, as well as the smartest, and I can't understand why guys aren't moving heaven and hell to be with you."

"Who says they're not?"

He ducks his head. "Fair point. I guess I don't know that they're not."

"Can I ask you a personal question?"

"Yes."

"Why do you always make yourself smaller around me?"

"It's not just you. I'm a big guy and I don't want to intimidate people with my size."

"Except on the football field?"

"Except on the football field."

I pat the chair next to me. He takes a seat, stretching his shoulders back, which only furthers my point. "To answer your question, I don't have a boyfriend because I intimidate men."

"Because you're so beautiful?"

"No, men covet beauty. A gorgeous wife would be an asset to most of them, but usually I'm smarter, more educated, richer and more successful. They say they want that, but the reality is they don't. No man wants to be outshined."

Aggie nods, his gaze set on something in the distance, his mind lost in private thoughts.

Have I said too much? Probably. It's one of my big problems—my mouth is always running.

"It's my looks or last name that attract men who try to push past their insecurities to convince me they love me. Too often they love-bomb me in an attempt to control me."

"Love-bomb. I know that term well. It's the only love I know, but you're too smart to fall victim to that."

"It has nothing to do with intelligence, Aggie. I have an excellent support system at home with two protective brothers who would sit me down whenever they saw toxic behavior. I'm sure if your family had seen it, recognized it and understood what they needed to do to protect you, they would've stepped in before it was too late. Have you called them?"

"Not yet. I'm still trying to figure out what I'm going to say. They had no idea what was going on between Ellen and me over the years. I never let them know I was unhappy, not even in high school."

"You should call and invite them to a game."

"Maybe once I get myself settled in my own place."

"Have you started looking?"

"No, but Declan said he'd rent me his place because he's looking to move into a house."

"Did he tell you why?" A big cheesy smile spreads across my lips.

Aggie grins back at me. "I know it's a secret, but yeah he did."

"Oh my God, Danny is the cutest little thing ever. Way cuter than Declan was as a five-year-old."

"You seem excited to be an aunt."

"I am. I'm going to spoil that little boy rotten."

"Do you—" he bites his lip and looks away "—want your own family someday?"

"If I find the right man, I think I do."

"A man who is not intimidated by you, not after your family name, and is okay with being outshined by you?"

Chapter Seven
Aggie

The bells over the front door ring at the same time that Gio parts the curtains separating us from the back room. I stand up just as my teammates, Jepson and Rex, walk in, both men speaking loudly as always.

"If we can get you scheduled for two weeks from now for a final fitting?" Gio opens an old school appointment book as I catch them heading my way out of the corner of my eye.

Deidre remains seated, her face placid, as if she's unconcerned about being seen with me. I guess I should take that as a good sign?

"Hey man. Are you finally replacing the suits Ellen turned into campfire kindling?" Jepson comes around the corner and slaps my shoulder, but his eyes instantly go to Deidre. I can tell by the way his gaze roams over her long legs that something stupid is about to come out of his mouth, my protective instinct to shut him down roaring to life.

Ill-placed possessiveness bands around my heart, but I have no business feeling that way about her. She's not mine to claim and she never will be.

Jepson quirks his eyebrow, a smirk playing upon his lips. "Nice, Aggie. Way to get over that bitch of an ex-wife."

"It's not like that and watch your mouth," I mutter, keeping my tone low, my fist clenching even though I know I'm not going to do anything with them.

"Is she a dancer from the club?" He ignores me, his mouth running on autopilot. Of course, he would think she was a dancer, because he only goes to gentlemen's clubs.

"Shut up before you say something you regret," I hiss.

Deidre stands up and smooths her skirt. "No, I'm not a dancer."

"That's too bad." He flashes her a smile. "You look familiar, though."

She narrows her eyes. "You know, Mr. Masters, you should spend less time fighting with your brother at strip clubs and more time at your charitable organization—you know the one you're required to donate time and resources to monthly?"

She offers her hand to Gio. "Are you done with us for the day?"

"Yes, Ms. Scott. I have everything I need."

"Great. I appreciate you getting us in at the last minute." Without giving Jepson a second glance, Deidre pushes past my teammates and walks out of the store.

"Oh, shit," Rex hisses. "Please tell me that's not our

boss's daughter."

Sighing, I turn to Gio to shake his hand. "Thank you for everything, Mr. Salvatori. I'll see you in a couple of weeks."

"Yes, sir. I'm looking forward to it."

My gaze snaps to Jepson and Rex. "This isn't what it looks like, and I don't want to hear about this in the locker room tomorrow."

They both shake their heads. "Nope. We never saw you."

"That works for me," I say as I walk out to find Deidre standing out front looking at the window of the high-end women's clothing store next door.

"He really is an ass."

"I think he and his brother had messed up childhoods and are working through some stuff."

"Yeah, well, the organization isn't going to put up with any more shenanigans from them, no matter how great they are on the field. But honestly, I shouldn't be discussing that with you."

"I'm sorry they saw you with me."

She brings her eyes up to mine. "What are you talking about? I'm not worried about people seeing us together. Are you?"

"No, but I definitely don't want rumors starting about me and the boss's daughter, if you know what I mean."

"Is that what I am to you? Your boss's daughter?"

I cast my eyes to the ground. "I don't know how to answer that."

Deidre flashes me a placating smile that doesn't reach

her eyes and switches her purse to her left hand, offering me her right. "Well, Mr Dunham, I think you have everything you need. Gio's going to take excellent care of you. His suits are the best, and you'll need them as I have no doubt you'll help carry the team to the championship game."

"Deidre. What do you want me to say?" I plead. I know I've upset her, but I don't know what I'm supposed to do here. What does she want from me, from us? What can there be between us?

She shakes her head, pulling her hand from mine. "Nothing, Aggie. I think we've said everything we need to say." Her smile widens to a camera-facing brilliance. "Now I need to get to the toy store so I can get my nephew something that makes him declare me the best aunt ever."

Watching her walk away, my gut ties up in knots. I don't know how to do this—flirt, date, admit feelings I'm not supposed to have, but do anyway. My instinct says to stay away from Deidre Scott. She's out of my league in every way, yet she consumes my thoughts and fills my dreams of a life beyond my wildest fantasies.

The tailor's front door opens behind me. "How much trouble am I in?" Jepson says softly.

I tear my gaze from her retreating form and look him dead in the eye. "In general, I'd say a lot. If you don't respect yourself, at least respect the jersey and the organization backing it. Your crap affects not only you, but everyone else who dances within your sphere of influence—specifically your brother. If you're going to self-destruct, do it away from the team and our championship season."

I expect him to explode—rant and rave and tell me how it's not his fault. That's what my ex would do. Instead, he surprises me by shoving his hands in his pockets and hanging his head low. "I'm trying, man. I just... I get stupid sometimes."

For the first time, I look past the pretty face into the torment clouding his dark blue eyes. "Do you have a therapist you can talk to?"

He drops his eyes to the ground. "Yeah."

I nod. "Good. I find talking to someone helpful."

"Oh, yeah?" He sounds surprised.

"Yeah, man. There's no shame in talking through your crap. I'm glad you're seeing someone."

"Well, I didn't have much of a choice. The coach ordered it a while ago."

"However you get there, showing up is what is important."

Rex walks out of the store with two suits slung over his shoulder. "You want to grab a burger with us, Aggie?"

I quirk my eyebrow. "Just a burger?"

"Juicy beef between two buns next to a side of fries and maybe a milkshake. Nothing else." Rex points to an upscale grille across the parking lot as if to emphasize his point. "We're laying low for a while. No more rowdy nights out until we win a championship ring."

I look into the eyes of two of our bigger troublemakers, seeing nothing but sincerity and temperance—at least for the moment. "Okay."

One week later, I'm driving downtown to check out Declan's condo. He's already found a child-friendly place to play house in until they can make a more permanent move into their forever home—whatever that means.

I pull up to the valet, the attendant greeting me by name. "Good evening, Mr. Dunham. Mr. Scott told us to expect you. If you go through the lobby to the elevator on the far left, the attendant will send you up."

"Thanks."

Passing a concierge and a security guard, both of whom nod a greeting, I meet the elevator attendant who sends me up to the fifteenth floor through the use of a keycard. The elevator is a straight shot to Declan's condo, which immediately feels too fancy for a country bumpkin like me.

The doors open to a large space encased in glass over-looking Pikes Peak, the closest fourteener we have to Spring City. It's just after sunset, so the outline of the mountain is barely visible with the last of the day's sun painting the sky in a palette of dark purples and midnight blues.

"Hey man." Declan smiles as he walks in from the hallway. "You want to meet my son?"

"Really?" He hasn't introduced Danny to the team, considering Deidre hasn't released the news to the press yet. But something tells me that is coming soon, as I think he's going crazy not being able to shout it from the rafters and she knows it.

"Yeah, man. We're putting him to bed now." Declan tilts his head, instructing me to follow him down the hall into one of the three bedrooms this massive condo has.

I really don't need something this big, but I want to move out of Devlin's house as soon as possible and the rental market in Spring City sucks right now. He hasn't said anything, nor has he made me feel uncomfortable about taking over his basement, but I'm pretty sure he's got a girlfriend—one he barely talks about and never brings to the house.

I'm cramping his style and overstaying my welcome, so it's time to move.

Amelia, the mother of Declan's child and his new fiancée, sits on the edge of a bed with a book in her hand. She stops reading and smiles up at us. "Hi there."

"I'm sorry to interrupt." I give the little blond-haired, blue-eyed boy a small wave of my hand.

"You're huge," he says with wide eyes.

"Danny," Amelia tsks. "Sorry. Five-year-olds rarely think before they speak."

"It's not a problem. I am a big guy." I smile at him.

"You protect my daddy on the football field, huh?"

"I try to."

"He's one of the best offensive tackles in the league, bud." Declan slaps my shoulder. "Together, we're going to win the championship."

"Yay!" Danny throws his hands up in the air. With

that energetic action, Amelia sighs and puts the book down, giving up on the bedtime story.

"You want to help Daddy give Uncle Aggie a tour of the condo?" Declan lifts Danny out of bed, letting the boy wrap his legs around his hips.

Amelia rolls her eyes and shakes her head. "You are dealing with him in the morning when he's all cranky."

"Not a problem, baby." Declan wraps his free arm around her waist and pulls her close, pressing a kiss to her neck. I've never seen him so happy or affectionate. Having a family looks good on him.

"I'm really sorry. I should have come earlier." Shoving my hands in my pockets, I take a step back into the hall.

"It's fine. Once Danny is down, he sleeps like the dead. Nothing wakes him up—" Declan waggles his brows "—and I do mean, nothing."

Amelia gasps, her cheeks turning a bright shade of pink, which also causes me to blush. "Declan!"

"Let's get this tour done so you can smack him around after I leave." I chuckle, casting my eyes to the ground.

She shakes her head, resting her hand on her round hips. "Maybe you should let a couple of defenders through next Sunday for me."

"I would, but I like my job, which requires me to protect him."

Declan chuckles and turns to Danny. "Which room should we show him first?"

"Ummm. Shaggy's room." Danny lifts his arms to me.

Before I understand what's going on, Declan is transferring his little boy into my arms and I'm carrying a five-year-old down the hallway to the third bedroom outfitted as an office / gaming room. A big sheepdog lifts her head from her bed—having slept through all the commotion—but one look at me and she jumps to her feet, tail wagging as she approaches. "Big dog. Are you sure you're okay with me bringing Rev here?"

"Sure. Anything a dog destroys can be fixed or replaced."

"Who watches Shaggy when we're out of town? I need to find a reliable sitter. Taking Rev to the kennel breaks my heart."

He shrugs. "Most of the time Mom and Deidre watch her. Occasionally, I have to hire a pet sitter. I can give you the name of a service."

"I didn't know Deidre liked dogs." Why did that comment need to slip out of my mouth?

He raises his brow but says nothing. "Three bedrooms, three bathrooms, more space than I think you need. All the furniture stays, unless you want it out. We can deal with that as needed. Here's the primary bedroom and the en-suite bath, as well as the walk-in closet. Didn't you go suit shopping the other day?"

"Uh..." Shoot, what does he know? Did Deidre tell him? She said she wasn't worried about being seen with me, but would she tell her brothers she's spending time with me? And if so, why haven't they killed me yet? "Yeah. I went to Salvatori's."

"Nice. Gio's the best. His family has been outfitting

us since my grandfather's heyday. A little thorough on the measurements, but the suits fit too well to complain."

We walk back into the living area. Danny has grown quiet, resting his head on my shoulder as we walk out onto a terrace overlooking the west side of the city. "Wow. This is beautiful."

"And the security is top-notch. You know, in case some crazy stalker type finds out you're living here and tries to come up." He casts me a knowing arch of his brow.

"I haven't heard from her in weeks, not since the divorce proceedings. Honestly, it makes me kind of nervous, not knowing where she is and what she's doing."

"I'm sure my sister is still having her tailed if she's in Spring City. Maybe you should ask her?"

A soft snore blows against my neck and I pull my head back to check out the sleeping form in my arms. "Wow. He really does sleep like the dead."

"Yeah." Declan leads me back to the smaller bedroom.

I gently lay the boy down and let Declan do the daddy thing, cocooning him with plush toys and turning down all the lights. "You've really taken to this whole fatherhood thing."

"Man, I feel like I was made for this shit." We walk back out to the kitchen. At some point, we lost Amelia. I think she's in the primary bedroom. Declan grabs a seltzer water out of the refrigerator and hands it to me. "I've never been so happy."

"It looks good on you. Amelia seems really nice." I pop the top and take a healthy swig.

"She's amazing. I'm in awe of her, raising our son on her own like she has. She's the feeling I've been chasing for the last six years. We met at a bad time. I was too immature to realize I'd met the best thing that was ever going to happen to me and I let her get away. But someone up there must really like me to give me a second chance, ya know?"

"What was the feeling you were chasing?"

"I didn't know until we reconnected, but it was peace. She brings me peace by making me feel whole when no one or anything else has come close. Don't get me wrong, I love my job and the game. I love the team and my teammates—you and Devlin are my best friends —and I love my parents and my siblings, but I always felt like there was something missing. I kept thinking maybe a new car would fill the hole? Or a week on a tropical beach? Or tele-skiing Whistler Mountain?" He lowers his voice, "Or sex with this woman or that woman."

He sighs. "None of it fills the hole like ten minutes with Amelia and Danny on a park bench does."

"That's great, man. I'm really happy for you."

"What about you?" Declan crosses his arms over his broad chest. "What's going on between you and Deidre?"

I sputter, spewing flavored seltzer water all over the kitchen island. "What?"

"I've seen how you look at her." His voice is even, and his expression is calm.

"Uh, there's nothing going on. She's an amazing

woman, but she's the boss's daughter, my best friend's sister, and—" I shake my head "—so far out of my league, I'd only embarrass myself by chasing after her."

He grabs a couple of paper towels and throws them at me. "I've been running off her douchebag boyfriends my whole life. Yes, Deidre is an exceptional woman. She's beautiful, rich, smart, and probably more driven to be the best than me and Deacon combined. It will take an exceptional man to win her heart. When she finds him, he won't have to fight her for it, because underneath that tough exterior is a woman who wants to be loved for her and all her ball-busting glory. She'll give him her heart freely."

Declan leans his hip against the counter, pounding his fist gently against the smooth black granite as he stares out the window into the darkness. "You're one of my best friends, Aggie. Ellen did a number on you and I'm not sure how many therapy sessions it's going to take to get your head screwed on right, but you should know the only person who doesn't think you are exceptional is you. Your opinion is the only thing holding you back from being in Deidre's league, as you call it."

I'm at a loss of how to respond. Is he giving me permission to pursue his sister? I think he is, but what does that mean in the big picture? She's still the boss's daughter.

He shakes his head and turns to face me, his eyes darting across the room as Amelia emerges from the bedroom. "So? When can you move in?"

Chapter Eight
Deidre

"You have a delivery." My assistant Becki pokes her head in my office with a big smile on her face. I've been keeping myself busy the last few weeks. After Deacon's engagement, which as I predicted is now on the back page of the Lifestyle section of most papers and blogs, there was the front-page worthy announcement of Declan's child and subsequent engagement—a hot topic on every Sunday football show. All of this is happening during the team's march toward the championship game —we have to win the next two games to clinch the division—so yeah, things are super busy in the home office. The Masters twins have kept SMZ entertained with their nightclub antics, enough home team drama to keep the producer happy and away from Ellen's domestic violence claims.

Considering the courtroom spectacle actress Amber Harrod had recently with a similar fraudulent claim, I don't think SMZ wants to risk another lawsuit, which we most definitely would pursue.

According to my investigator, Ellen has been laying low. She left town after the divorce but has come back several times for long weekends, placing all her stuff from the house in storage. It sold quickly, which means Aggie is now truly free and clear of Ms. Ellen Whitham.

Of course, I haven't talked to him in weeks. My heart aches and my feelings are hurt, but I guess it's better to know now—he's not in the right place to be with someone who won't chase after or gaslight him into loving them—than learn the hard lesson months from now after my heart is fully invested.

Besides... he needs time to play the field, sow his wild oats, and notch his bedpost before he settles down again, while I'm in the market for a committed relationship.

At least that's what I keep telling myself.

"What is it?" I stand, using the distraction as an excuse to stretch my limbs.

She pushes the door open and pulls in a cart full of flowers behind her.

"What the hell? Who died, because it's not my birthday?"

Becki places four bouquets on my side table, each one more elaborate than the next. "Someone sent these anonymously. The only instruction the delivery guy had is you're supposed to read the cards in order, starting with #1."

Card #1 is stuck in the simplest bouquet comprised of rustic wildflowers and white daisies.

"I'll leave you to your mystery." She giggles, pushing the cart out and closing the door behind her.

"Thanks." I call back absentmindedly, my brain cycling through who from my past would do something like this. Men who send me flowers typically default to a dozen long-stemmed red roses with baby's breath in a long gold box with maybe a sprig of crystals or something. They are never original, never eye-catching like these assortments before me.

I slide my letter opener under the flap and pull out a thick square of card stock.

I woke up on a Monday, my heart light and soul free, my thoughts with a beautiful woman who gifted me a new life with two phone calls and a handshake. We met for lunch. Was it business or friendship—perhaps a bit of both—but when I drove up your driveway and was greeted by a vision in emerald green, I had two thoughts. One: what would it be like to come home to you every day? And two: I wish I had brought you flowers. Better yet, I wish I could have stopped in a field and picked them for you myself, making sure each bloom was absolutely perfect, like you.

Fingering sprigs of rosemary and eucalyptus, I let out a shaky breath and pull card #2 out of the second bouquet, which is whimsical compared to the others. It's a collection of white and yellow daisies with sunflowers and white roses in a tall vase with tiny bumble bees on sticks, one of which has a T-shirt on that says, "*Be my Friend.*"

> *You offered me friendship. You said you wanted to be my ally. Both of which I want desperately. The problem is, sweet Deidre, I don't know how to be friends with a woman. I've never had one before. Can a man be purely friends with a woman he's attracted to? I honestly don't know. You're the most amazing woman I've ever met, so of course I'm enamored with your outer shell, but I'm also captivated by your inner beauty. You're tough, but you're also soft—ready to fight for those you love, but also those you barely know. Only a loving heart cares about people they don't know and I know you care about me. What I didn't know is why?*

I grab the card off the third bouquet—white lilies, roses and tulips—and wonder where this story is going. What is he trying to tell me? Is he ready to make a move? I mean, I love this. This is low-key romantic, which is absolutely warranted considering everything that has happened to him this season, but still. What is this?

> *I'm done worrying that I'm not good enough for you, because you're smart enough to decide*

that for yourself. I'd like to be friends, but honestly, I'd rather be more, because I don't think I'll be able to step back from another intense moment with you. The next time you look up at me with anything akin to need, I won't back down. I told you I prefer stolen moments. I fantasize about passing you in a hallway and pulling you into a closet, pushing you against the wall and kissing you breathless, until we're both too dazed to walk a straight line.

I reread this card multiple times, my stomach tightening and pussy clenching. Could the big, sweet, shy marshmallow have a dominant side? A primal need to take control in the bedroom? That's my ultimate dream, a man consumed with me who also knows how to let me run my professional life. I'm too much of a ball-buster to cower to a man in public, but private? That's a different fantasy.

The last card is with a dozen pink roses with red tips. I open the card and smile.

I want to see you. I'm tired of waiting for my feelings to subside. They aren't going anywhere, so it's time to face whatever this is between us and see where it goes.

I take all four cards and slide into my seat, rereading

them multiple times while the butterflies in my belly dance with excitement. Men have approached me in multiple ways since I was a teenager, some direct, some attempting to be clever or memorable, but this is the best request for a date I've ever received.

My phone dings with an incoming text.

Hello, Buster.

I bite my lip and giggle.

You know my family nickname

I've been informed. Do you like the flowers?

I do, but I like your words more.

Did you hear I moved into Declan's condo last week?

I did.

I'm cooking you dinner tonight. What time can you be here?

Oh god, I'm pretty sure that one declarative statement alone makes my clit throb. Nodding to no one, I'm telling him yes, giving him whatever he wants with unbridled enthusiasm, my only thought being, I have to get to him. I glance at the clock on my computer and then my full email box.

But what is he going to teach me?

I arrive at SC Towers, an ultra-posh, highly secure fifteen-story condo downtown. The valet takes my keys and smiles with a tilt of his head. John, the concierge, and Dave, the security guy, both furrow their brows as my heels click against the marble floor.

"Good evening, Ms. Scott. You know your brother moved out?"

"Yes, John. I know. I'm here to see Mr. Dunham. He's expecting me."

"He didn't call down," Dave frowns. That's what's so great about this place. Even though these guys know me and have for years, they don't let up on their security protocols. If Aggie didn't want me in the building, I wouldn't be here, no matter how much money my family has.

"Does he understand all the rules?" I raise my brow at Dave, who shrugs as his response.

John is already on the phone. "Yes, Mr. Dunham. We'll send her right up. We'll add her to your permanent list along with Mr. Scott and Mr. Frank."

"Thanks gentlemen," I say as I walk over to the elevator attendant who smiles and sends me up to the condo I helped Declan find five years ago. Hell, I'm practically the one who decorated it, with the help of a designer, because he was too busy to care.

"Make it hot," was his only contribution.

The doors open to a mouthwatering aroma as a small silver and black dog reminiscent of a plush animal runs up to greet me.

"Come on in," Aggie says from the kitchen. "I think you know your way around."

"Who is this?" I say, my hands full as I walk around the corner with a bottle of wine in one hand and the rustic wildflowers in the other.

"Oh, that's Reveille, but I call her Rev."

"Texas A&M Reveille, Aggie?"

He looks over his shoulder, flashing me a bashful grin. "Too cheesy?"

I set the bottle of wine and the flowers on the counter and bend down, picking up the furry love-monger who instantly cuddles herself up against my breasts. "Awww. She's so sweet."

"Yeah, she's my snuggle bug." He turns from the oven, sliding off a pair of oven mitts. "Are you hungry?"

"It smells amazing."

"Is lasagna okay?"

"Sounds great." This is so weird. Part of me wants to rush into his arms, part of me is unsure of my next step—which is unlike me. Usually I'm overly confident in pretty much everything I do, but something about his notes have me off-kilter.

One thing I know: I want him to drive this train, and I'm afraid I'll take control subconsciously and ruin the moment.

His gaze travels over my body purposefully. True to his word, he's not hiding from his feelings anymore. Smiling, he walks around the island and grabs the wine bottle and then leans forward to press a kiss against my cheek. "You look beautiful."

"Thank you."

"Shall I pour you a glass?" He lifts the bottle and walks over to the drawer where Declan kept the corkscrews, pulling out a goblet from the cabinet above.

"Did Declan leave everything behind?" I set Rev down, watching as she runs back to her bed near the couch to curl up into a furry ball.

"Besides his clothes, bedding, computers and bathroom stuff—yeah. He also took his mattress, but left the frame. Otherwise, he wants Amelia to pick out everything for their new life together. Considering I didn't take any of this stuff from my house, it works out well." He's wearing a button-down shirt, the collar open around his throat exposing the top of his muscular chest and black slacks that fit his thick thighs perfectly. He's a big man, bigger than any man I've ever been with, but I've fantasized about snuggling up on his chest while we watch the nightly news.

Or as I blissfully float down from a full body orgasm.

Either way.

He hands me the glass. "Thank you for coming tonight."

"How could I not after receiving your notes?"

He chuckles and pulls out a barstool for me at the island. "I wasn't sure how those were going to go over. I'm betting you've gotten plenty of love letters over the years, but those are the first I've ever written."

"Ever?" I perch on the stool, watching as he pulls an antipasto platter out of the refrigerator and sets it down on the island in front of me.

"I've never done this before, Deidre. I've never flirted, dated, or held eye contact for more than a few seconds." He offers me a piece of melon wrapped in prosciutto. I part my lips and let him feed me, watching as his soft brown eyes turn dark with desire.

"You're doing great," I say with a breathy voice as I hold still, like alert prey waiting for the predator to make their move.

"Yeah?" He grins and moves closer, his thighs brushing the tops of my knees.

I make a barely perceptible nod.

"I'm not moving too fast or coming on too strong?" Aggie leans forward, his forehead brushing the loose hairs on my head, his warm breath on my cheek.

I tilt my face up, unwilling to back down, but not closing the gap between us either.

He needs to do this.

I need him to do this.

My insides tingle and scream *Dear God, please kiss me*, but I say nothing, letting my lips part slightly in invitation as my only form of communication.

He reaches out and slides his fingers into my hair, cupping the back of my head. "Silky and soft, just like I thought it would be."

Oh my God, it's killing me not to break this tension and the distance between us. Holding still is not part of my skill set and patience has never been one of my virtues.

Sliding his thumb over my bottom lip, he tilts my head back and presses his lips gently to mine. I exhale the breath I've been holding, not just for the last several seconds, but for what feels like weeks / months / years. Closing my eyes, I turn into putty in his hands, my jaw lax and lips parting further as he runs his tongue along the seam of my mouth.

Without effort, he pulls me to my feet, sliding his free hand around my hip and over the small of my back, pulling me flush against his broad body.

I moan softly, sliding my fingers up his thick arms and over his pectorals as he deepens the kiss, his tongue warm and slick as it massages mine, exploring me tentatively and then purposefully until we're lost in the embrace.

The bell on the oven dings, pulling us out of this moment with a rudeness that annoys me. Aggie pulls back slightly, resting his forehead against mine. "Does it make me an unconscionable ass to say I've wondered what that would be like for years?"

"Maybe, but you barely made eye contact with me the few times we met over the years, and considering I was crushing on someone I couldn't have too, I guess we're both wrong."

Chapter Nine
Aggie

"That someone is me, right?" I smile and release her, the oven alarm showing no signs of giving up its onslaught.

She nods.

"Good." I turn off the alarm and the oven and open the door, letting the heat vent out into the kitchen. It's early December, and it's slated to snow later tonight, the first time since I moved into this condo. I'm betting the views of the city and mountains as snow falls will be beautiful, but not as breathtaking as the woman sitting with me.

I can't believe I just kissed Deidre Scott.

I wasn't kidding when I said I've been waiting years to do that. Well, maybe not waiting. I never would've crossed the line while married, no matter how unhappy I was, but I can say Deidre is the only woman I've ever had those kinds of thoughts about—which is crazy considering we spent little to no time together. Sure, I'd see her at team

BBQs, charity events and the occasional team butt-chewing when she would accompany the GM, the team lawyer and the coach to school us over some stupid public embarrassment someone did, but we've never really talked.

No. I liked the way she carried herself. Strong and self-assured, but not mean and never a bully—at least not when I was watching.

I pull the lasagna out of the oven and then the garlic bread, oblivious until this second that the meal I prepared and kissing are in dire opposition to each other.

Well, crap. I wonder if I have any gum?

"It smells amazing. Where did you learn to cook?"

I blush. "I took quite a few nutrition classes in college. My teacher liked to cook and would take us to local restaurants to learn. I have a knack for it and it came easy to me."

"Mmmm. How exciting. You know I love to eat." She takes a sip of her wine and walks over to the windows overlooking the mountains. "Do you like the condo?"

"It's a little too fancy for me, but I like it," I say as I make up two plates of lasagna, salad and bread.

"I picked it out, you know," she says. "I really like the area, and if Declan hadn't taken it, I probably would've."

"Oh yeah? Are you saying you want to move in?" I set our plates on the glass dining room table.

She smiles and shakes her head, taking her seat at the table. "Maybe after our third date. I don't want to pull a stunt like my brothers and start a family after one night."

I refill her wineglass and then sit in the chair next to

her. "They are pretty crazy, but you know, I've never seen Declan happier. I mean, I thought he was happy before, but that was nothing like he is now. He loves that little boy and Amelia something fierce. Do you think falling in love overnight like that is possible?"

She shrugs, picking up her fork and cutting into her lasagna. "If it hadn't happened to my brother—Mr. Bachelor himself—I'd say no. But Declan couldn't—no, he wouldn't—fake something like that. So I guess it's possible."

I wait for her to take her first bite, blood rushing to my cock as her lips wrap around the fork, her eyes flutter close and she lets out a guttural moan. "Oh, this is so good."

Whoa. I had no idea watching a woman eat could be so erotic. Is she purposefully being provocative or is she having a visceral reaction to the food? Either way, I could sit here and watch her eat all night.

"Did you use fresh basil in this?" She presses her lips together as if to savor the memory of her first bite.

"Fresh basil. Fresh everything."

"You made the sauce from scratch?"

"Of course."

She takes another bite, this one bigger, her eyes closed as she smiles and chews thoughtfully. "Forgive me while I make a pig of myself."

Chuckling, I take a bite. "I'll have to cook for you more often."

"Anytime you want to cook for me, call me."

"Tomorrow night?" I throw out there with a wry smile on my face.

She takes a sip of her wine and looks me dead in the eye. "Or in the morning."

I don't respond to that. I can't. There's no blood left in my brain.

She smiles and drops her gaze to her plate. "Can I ask you something?"

"Yes."

"Why did you change your mind about us? What made you finally send the notes?"

I not only expected her to ask this, I hoped she would. "It was something your brother said a few weeks ago. The timing of the notes... well, I had to have my own place before I asked you out. Cooking for you in Devlin's kitchen while living in his basement was not an option."

"That makes sense, although you could have offered to make me dinner at my house." She takes another sip of her wine. "What did my brother say?"

I put my fork down and offer her my hand, waiting until she sets down her wineglass and takes it. "He said the only person who doesn't think I'm exceptional is me and that it will take an exceptional man to win your heart."

"You want to win my heart?" She cocks her brow in surprise.

"I do." I rub my thumb over the back of her hand and then lift it to my mouth, placing a gentle kiss against her knuckles.

She sucks in her breath, watching my every move. Her voice is breathy as she asks, "By being exceptional?"

"By being exactly the man you need."

Pressing her lips together, her gaze drifts to the windows where light snow flurries on a strong wind beat against the glass. "How well will the lasagna reheat?"

"Very well, why?"

"Maybe you should show me what kind of man I need and we can eat later after we've worked up an appetite?"

You wouldn't think a man my size can move fast, but when I'm motivated, I'm quite agile. I stand and pull her to her feet, walking around the table to the living area and the oversized leather couch. Pulling her onto my lap, I have my hand in her hair and my lips on hers before she can utter an objection.

Not that I think she would.

Deidre melts into me, kicking off her high heels and pulling her feet up on the cushion, turning her lithe body into mine. I pull a blanket off the back of the couch and drape it over her bare legs, never once releasing her mouth, my tongue plunging in and tangling with hers. She's wearing a gray pencil skirt that hits mid-knee and a soft cashmere sweater loose enough that I easily slide my hand under it to caress her warm, taut stomach.

She moans, encouraging my touch as I move up, cupping her lace-covered breasts with their tight pebbled nipples.

Sweet Jesus, I'm going to come in my pants if we don't slow this down. It's been a long time since I've had sex—eight months if I'm counting correctly, and before that it was rare—and I don't think I've ever been this turned on.

She arches into my touch, throwing her head back and exposing her neck for me to trail kisses down. I pull at her sweater and murmur against her skin, "I want this off."

Deidre pushes against my chest and crawls off my lap to stand up, pulling her sweater over her head.

I suck in my breath as she tosses it onto the cushion next to me.

"What else do you want?" Standing confidently in a lacy pink bra, she offers me a knowing cock of her brow.

I hear the subtext. She doesn't want me to ask and definitely not to beg. Deidre wants me to take control, and that I can do. Leaning forward, I slide my hands over the sides of her hips to the zipper of her skirt. I keep my eyes on hers as I slip the zipper down and let her skirt fall to her feet, which I lift one at a time so I can lay her skirt on top of her sweater. Wrapping my big palms around her hips, I push her back a couple steps and drop to my knees in front of her, running my hands down her long muscular legs and then back up her quads, pressing my thumbs along the insides of her thighs.

Her breathing changes slightly, her beautiful aqua eyes bright as she watches me.

"Put your hands on my shoulders," I instruct.

She places her delicate fingers on me as I prod her legs apart, pressing my lips to her inner thigh. I inhale deeply, her arousal like sweet ambrosia. She's pure perfection, every inch of her from the top of her head to the tips of her painted toes.

A low groan comes from my throat as I press my face against her lace-clad pussy, my thumbs skimming the edges of her panties, pulling her skin tight and her lower lips apart as I stroke her with the tip of my nose.

Deidre's breathing grows shallow as she squeezes my shoulders. "Do you plan to tease me all night?"

I look up at her. "No, babe. I plan to savor you."

Chapter Ten
Deidre

Savor. His words bounce around in my head as he slowly glides my panties down my legs. He lifts my left foot and places it on his right thigh, spreading me wide enough that the first swipe of his tongue hits my clit perfectly, my eyes fluttering closed as a low whimper escapes my lips.

"Sweet perfection," he whispers, his tongue flicking the bundle of nerves until my hips are involuntarily bucking against his face, seeking my pleasure from his talented mouth.

His fingers dig into my ass as he alternates between licking and sucking, both actions bringing me quickly to the edge.

"Oh, God—" I gasp "—I'm so close."

My words unravel his control. He stands and swings me up into his arms, carrying me into his bedroom without speaking a word. His reserved silence only intensifies the dominance with which he handles me. Tossing me on his bed, he descends with fluid grace, his mouth on me before my building climax can lose momentum. He spreads my thighs wide, licking and sucking until I am arching my back and lifting my hips, riding his mouth and splintering into a million pieces.

I cry out my release, my entire body zinging to life and tingling with tiny electrical shocks spreading through my limbs.

Aggie slows down his tongue, but doesn't remove his mouth from me, letting me ride wave after wave of pleasure as it courses through my body. He presses gentle kisses to my thighs, landing languid licks to my pussy, my sensitive clit causing my hips to jerk and thigh muscles to clench.

"I like the way you come." His voice is rich and velvety smooth, like decadent chocolate.

I stretch my arms out, running my fingers over his silky cotton duvet. "I like the way you make me come."

He chuckles, moving my legs to his side as he crawls up the bed to lie beside me. His fingers dance over my skin and up my belly until he's deftly unclasping the front of my bra, separating the cups to put my breasts on display. His normally soft brown eyes are dark as he lowers his head and sucks my nipple between his lips.

I run my fingers through his thick hair, scraping my nails against his scalp, silently begging him to kiss me again.

"You have me stripped bare and yet you have all of your clothes on, even your shoes."

Aggie lifts his head to meet my eyes, the tale-telling

sound of shoes dropping on the carpeted floor taunting me.

"That's one piece of clothing." I slide my hand over his hard, muscled chest and pop open a button and then another, his hand sliding down my body the lower I move on his shirt. When I reach for the buttons on his slacks, he slides his hand between my legs, the slight touch of his finger over my clit causing my legs to spread wantonly for him.

He grins as if he knows exactly how eager I am for him, but says nothing.

His quiet confidence is sexy, more erotic than if he was telling me in detail all he wants to do to me—and I thought that would be the ultimate high I would receive from him.

His eyes flutter closed the moment I slide my hand over his thick cock pressed angrily against the seam of his zipper. He's big—everywhere—causing me to suck in my breath. "Oh, Aggie."

He chuckles again, opening his eyes that are near black with need. "Did you expect any different?"

"I didn't know what to expect." I bite my lip as he slides two fingers inside me. "You need to get your clothes off."

"Not yet." His touch is unhurried, his fingers slow and steady as he pumps in and out of me while pressing the heel of his palm against my clit. It takes no time until I've forgotten about playing with him, my hips and ass coming off the mattress to ride his hand to another climax.

He latches on to my nipple as I come apart, gripping the duvet in balled up fists as I come. "Fuck me." I pant, my cunt convulsing and flooding with arousal.

"So pretty when you come." I open my eyes to find him staring down at me, an amused smirk on his lips.

"You like having control over my body, don't you?"

"Yeah, I do." He brings his fingers up to his mouth and sucks them clean.

My jaw drops. "That is unbelievably hot."

"I can't waste any of it. It's like pouring expensive champagne down the drain—you don't."

My always-has-to-get-the-last-word-in competitive side wants to point out that you do when the champagne goes bad, but I keep that to myself, since it doesn't prove his point. "You were undressing."

"Was I?"

"Teasing me some more?"

"Savoring, beautiful. With you, I'm always savoring."

I roll him to his back and push up onto my knees beside him. He adjusts, one hand going behind his head, his huge bicep stretching the fabric of his shirt tight, the other caressing my hip.

Pulling his shirt free from his pants, I push the sides off of his wide chest and stare down at him with a sense of awe. "You are magnificent. We should get you a Men's Fitness cover deal or something."

He shakes his head. "Not my style, plus there are plenty of guys on the team way more ripped than me."

"Still, women would swoon over a picture of this." I

trail my fingers over his pecs and abs, his nipples pebbling under my attention.

"You'd flaunt me to the world?"

"Why not?"

He shrugs. "My ex was insanely jealous. She didn't want me taking off my shirt at practice, the gym, nothing."

"I'm not insecure. If you were mine, I wouldn't care who is looking at you."

"I am yours."

Goosebumps rise on my skin with his words, but I shake my head to knock them out before they take root, grow and wrap tendrils around my heart. "You're single for the first time in forever, Aggie. You don't have to make a commitment to me. I'm sure you'll want to play around before getting into another relationship."

His brow furrows, and he grabs my hand, pulling me down on top of him, our lips inches apart, gazes locked onto each other. "I'm not a play around kind of guy, Deidre. No, I've never been single before, but I also haven't lived my life fantasizing about all the tail I could chase either. That's not me. Should I want to play the field? Maybe. But why would I when I already have my hands on what I want?"

I let out a shaky breath. "I'm only saying, I'd understand if you don't want to get serious right away."

He slides his hand into my hair. "I'm not Ivy League educated, Deidre, and I get knocked in the head often, but I'm not stupid enough to think a guy like me gets more than one chance with you. I'm a one-woman man and you're the woman I want. Understood?"

I close my eyes and press my lips to his. "Please get naked with me."

"I can do that." He slides off the bed and pulls off his shirt, letting his slacks drop to the ground. He's a boxers kind of guy, his hard cock jutting out of the top and glistening with pre-cum, the vision of both him and his readiness making my mouth water.

I get on my hands and knees and crawl to the edge of the bed, looking up at him like a parched woman in the middle of the desert. "I want you in my mouth."

Now it's his turn to let out a shaky breath. "It's been a long time, babe. If you take me between your luscious lips, I'm not going to be able to control myself."

"I'd like to see you lose control." I reach out and wrap my fingers around his impressive erection, both long and thick. Leaning down, I swipe at the pre-cum with my tongue and then open my mouth wide, taking him as deep as I can.

He groans and threads his fingers through my hair. "Oh, damn."

"Mmhmmm," I moan, letting the vibration heighten his pleasure, sliding him in and out of my mouth until his fingers tighten and he pulls me off of him. He pops his cock free from my mouth, and I lick my lips as I look up and meet his eyes. "Everything okay?"

"As I said, it's been a while and I'm not ready to come yet."

I roll back onto my ass, set my feet on the mattress

with my legs spread and look down at him standing at the edge of the bed. "How do you want me, Ags?"

His eyes heat as he lets them slowly trail over my body. The only movement he makes is to push his boxers off and set one knee on the edge of the bed. "You are, by far, the most perfect woman I've ever met." He starts at my knees and then slides his hands down my thighs and over my hips, picking me up and pulling me toward him until my ass is at the edge of the bed.

"I hope you plan to stay the night because this first time will go fast, but I plan to make it up to you until daybreak."

"I'll stay as long as you need me."

"I need you. I also want you, in equal measure."

"Why?" I tease him, smiling and running my hands up his forearms as he leans forward and puts his nose to mine, pressing soft kisses to my lips.

"Because with you I feel like I can breathe. You're the oxygen the air has been missing."

His hand is between our bodies, his thumb circling my clit as he lines up the head of his cock. The crown pushes against me, breaching me like a virgin and not a thirty-year-old woman with a collection of vibrators.

"Ah," I gasp, his size stretching me no matter how gently he takes me.

"I'm sorry." The veins in his neck stand out as he tries to control himself.

I lift my legs, wrapping one high on his back, the other behind his thighs, coaxing him to push in and fully seat himself. He does and my pussy pulses around him, my body on the verge of climaxing—much to my surprise.

Aggie has his eyes closed, his forehead resting against mine, and I swear he's counting backwards. "Damn, you feel so good."

"Mmhmmm." I trail my fingers up and down his massive arms, waiting for him to move and send me over the edge. I know he will. He fits me perfectly, overfills me, touching every nook and cranny, my orgasm unable to hide when he's inside me. The words he says keep my mind on edge.

He pulls back, sliding his delicious length out inch by glorious inch, and colors pop behind my eyes. I toss my head, tilt my chin in the air and give myself over as Aggie works himself in and out of me at a slow, teasing, torturous pace. He nuzzles my neck and hisses sweetness into my ear. "You are the filter that pulls the toxins from my blood. The balm that soothes my soul. The water that gives me life. You are everything I've wanted and dreamed I'd never have. I'm going to make love to you nightly, even when we are physically apart, until you tell me you no longer want my love and then, I'm going to convince you why you need it."

"I had no idea you were a poet."

He lifts his head, his hips moving a little faster now, his eyes hooded and love drunk. "I wasn't until you."

My climax teeters on the edge and comes crashing over with those four words. It starts off gentle and then becomes a total body release as I dig my fingers into his biceps. My cunt clamps down on him, causing him to lose control, his hips moving faster as he chases his release. He pulls out at the last minute, shooting his seed into the boxer shorts I hadn't realized he put on the bed besides us.

I let my head fall back, my hands dropping from his arms. "I should have told you, I have the ring. You can come inside me."

"That's good to know, otherwise I'll be doing a lot of laundry." He scoops me up in his arms and repositions me on the bed with my head resting against the pillows, pulling the duvet down and then sliding in beside me, the night sky bespectacled with light fluffy snowflakes. Aggie wraps me in his arms and pulls me against his warm chest. "We have a lot to talk about."

"Like what?" His words have an ominous tone.

"What you like, dislike, fantasize about—all the things I need to know."

I chuckle. "I thought you were getting serious on me."

"I am serious. I want to please you."

"What about my need to please you?"

"You do, babe. Didn't I tell you I'm a simple man? Holding you in my arms is very pleasing. Being inside you again in ten minutes will make me even happier."

"Ten minutes?" I arch my brow and slide my hand between us, his soft cock rousing in my palm.

"Touch me like that and it's five."

"Sounds like we have a fun night ahead of us."

"This time you'll ride me and show me how you like it." He cups my face, his gentle full lips hard as he takes me this time, rolling on to his back and moving me to where I'm straddling him. I feel his kiss in my toes, but this isn't about exploration this time; this is about possession.

Arnold Aggie Dunham wants to claim me as his own, and I'm down for it.

Chapter Eleven
Aggie

We made love all night and into the morning, and I found Deidre is just as insatiable as I am. Our bodies fit together perfectly, and she assuaged any concerns I had about being too big or too heavy for her. She took me everywhere I wanted to take her and a few ways I've never tried before and I'm willing to spend the entire weekend in this bed if that's what she wants.

Thank God we have a bye this Sunday.

I wake up alone in my bed, but her side is warm, so I know she's nearby.

Seconds later, she walks into the bedroom wearing my shirt from last night; the buttons undone sans one fastened right between her breasts. Seeing her wearing my shirt has to be the sexiest thing I've ever seen—way better than babydoll lingerie and lacy thongs.

When I drag my eyes up to meet hers, I find her brow furrowed. "You don't have any coffee."

"Uh, no. I rarely drink it, but I'll rectify that problem today."

"Oh yes. This isn't going to work if you don't have coffee." She crawls back into bed and snuggles up on my chest. "There's an amazing European cafe around the corner with the best coffee and pastries in Spring City."

"Sounds like we're going there."

"Before or after a shower?"

"We showered a few hours ago. Do you think we need another one so soon?"

She trails her fingers up and down my chest, her hand dipping a little lower with every pass. "I smell like you, but I like it."

"Really? I think I smell like you."

Giggling, she kisses my jaw. "I'm sure you do."

"That settles it. No shower this morning." I kiss the top of her head, rubbing my hand over the globe of her perfect ass cheek.

"What am I going to wear to the cafe?" she says jokingly.

"Exactly what you are wearing right now."

"People will talk."

I shrug. "After last night, I'm too happy to care what people say about me."

She squeezes my chest and then lifts to look me in the eye. "Seriously. Coffee. Now."

"Oh?" I grip her ass and pull her on top of me. She straddles my waist, which causes my cock to harden at her heat and wetness. "This is a thing. A genuine coffee addiction?"

Deidre closes her eyes and smiles. "You're teasing again."

"Distracting and savoring, babe."

"Okay, but then coffee."

"Yes, ma'am."

Twenty minutes later, a quick rinse in the shower—because we got very dirty—and we exit the elevator hand in hand. She's wearing my shirt and her skirt, sans bra and panties per my request. Her heels are impractical in the snow, but she says we're connected to the cafe via a sidewalk that is well-maintained. The snow stopped falling in the early morning hours, and luckily she has her thick cashmere coat on with my scarf wrapped loosely around her neck.

The morning concierge and security guards look up as the elevator doors ding, the expression on their faces letting me know Deidre is acquainted with them and vice versa. Although they keep it professional, limiting the shock and speculation on their faces to the bare minimum, it's there.

"Good morning Mr. Dunham. Ms. Scott."

"Hi Bill, Tom." Deidre smiles, nods in their direction and keeps walking forward, completely unfazed by their attention.

We walk through the front door and turn left, passing the valet and another security guard when a banshee scream rips through the quiet, picturesque morning sky.

"I fucking knew it!"

Out of the corner of my eye, I see a red metal tumbler fly toward us. Instinctively, I pull Deidre into my chest and wrap my arms around her in a protective embrace.

A slight sting burns the exposed flesh of my hand, and then chaos ensues. Colder liquid dumps on Deidre's head and splashes me in the face as we're rushed back inside by bodies that move hard and fast like professional football players.

"What the fuck?" Deidre tries to pull out of my arms, but I'm unwilling or unable to let go.

The shrieking continues, my brain connecting and recognizing the high-pitched voice behind one of Ellen's tantrums. "Get off me your fucking prick! I'll kill you and your whore!"

Another one of the security guards has Ellen in a bear hug as she kicks and flails in the lobby only ten feet away from us.

"Are you out of your mind?" I growl, finally loosening my grip on Deidre to pull back and look at her. She's soaked, her hair matted, but there's no blood, just red, tender flesh down her neck and on the side of her face.

Bill, the concierge, is pushing us into a small office behind his desk, pulling on Deidre's jacket. "We have to get this clothing off you, Ms. Scott."

"What are you doing?" My mind spins.

"I think the woman poured acid on you. We have to get your clothing away from your skin."

Deidre and I yank on her jacket and scarf, pulling them off and tossing them to the ground. I rip open her shirt—my shirt—only to remember she's not wearing anything underneath. Deidre doesn't seem to care, yanking it off to stand topless in the room with no windows and only one observer that I'd rather not see my woman this way. I also shed my jacket and then tentatively cup her face near the irritated skin.

"Here." Bill gives me another bottle of water and puts a trash can and Deidre's feet. "Flush her hair and skin, just in case Tom didn't get it off her when he doused you out there. It will help neutralize the acid."

"How the hell do you know that?"

"I used to be a combat medic."

Deidre bends forward, her arms covering her breasts, and I pour water over the side of her face, jostling her hair which falls off in a clump in my hand. "Oh, shit."

She takes the handful of silky soft blonde hair from me, her body shaking, but says nothing.

"We need something to wrap around her."

"Here's a blanket from the concierge desk." Bill hands it to me. "We have EMS on their way."

"Are you okay?" I tilt her face up to mine, expecting tears.

Her teeth are chattering, but her eyes are bright, her pupils dilated. "She's fucking crazy."

"Yeah."

"I'm pressing charges, Aggie."

I nod. "Yes."

I can't say anything more. I'm in too much shock to

comprehend this. Ellen could be violent with me; I knew that. She's come at me too many times over the years and has even been arrested a few times—although I never pressed charges—but I never in a million years thought she'd go this far.

While EMTs enter the near soundproof room, Ellen's screams pierce the air as she's being handcuffed by two police officers. "Aggie! Don't let them do this to me!"

While the EMTs check out Deidre's neck, one of the officers enters the room. "I suppose you're pressing charges?"

"Oh, you're damn right!" Deidre hisses. "Throwing acid is a violent assault with intent to maim or disfigure and carries a ten-year prison sentence, minimum."

"Yes, ma'am. She's claiming you're with her husband?" he mumbles, as if he knows it's a ludicrous thing to say. Nothing can justify what Ellen just did. Nothing.

"Ex-husband," I say.

He nods. "Well, she also took a swing at my partner, so we'll tack on aggravated assault of a police officer."

"And she violated the restraining order." I sigh, standing back as the EMTs discuss the burns on Deidre's neck. My gut tightens into a ball of dread as I watch my woman's eyes search the ground, holding back tears—of anger or pain, maybe both, I'm unsure. All I know is she's not looking at me.

"You have a restraining order against her? We'll need to take your statement, sir."

"Can I come by later?" I glance at Deidre.

He nods again and hands me a card. "If you could give me your name and cell, I'll call you with her intake number as soon as we process her."

"Sure." I rattle off my information and slide his card into my back pocket. "Call you in a few hours."

He leaves and Ellen is still screaming at the top of her lungs, calling my name, as they escort her out of the building.

"We're ready to go," the EMT says.

"I don't need an ambulance." Deidre finally lifts her eyes to me.

"It's your choice, ma'am, but we highly suggest letting us take you in."

"Baby, let's take the ride so they get us right into the room."

She shakes her head. "Fine, but I'm calling my doctor on the way."

"Sounds good." The EMT escorts her out as I grab her coat, pulling her phone and wallet out of the pocket.

I give Bill an apologetic, if not exasperated look.

He nods and pats my arm as if I don't have to explain. "We have it, Mr. Dunham. We'll bag all the clothes, as I'm sure it will be evidence you'll need to hand over to the police."

"I'm sorry this happened, guys." I glance at the security guard, Tom, and another guy whose name I've yet to learn. Actually, he was the one who held Ellen in a bear hug.

"This is what we're here for, sir."

"You're here to deal with psycho exes?"

The big nameless guy shrugs. "This is one of the most secure buildings in the city, and we've been watching her since you moved in last week."

"What?" How could I not know she was following me?

"We didn't want to alarm you, but she's tried to gain entry multiple times," Bill adds.

"I'm only sorry we didn't recognize the cup as more than coffee before she attacked."

"That's why you were on us before I knew what was going on?" I guess.

"Yes, sir."

I rub my hand down my face, a few sensitive spots irritated by the rough handling of my cheek. "I've got to go, but I'll need your names for the police report."

"The officer already has our information, but we'll jot it down for you, too."

I nod and rush out of the room, the EMTs in the process of closing the back doors. "Can I ride with you?"

"Yes, sir."

Sitting next to Deidre, I slide my fingers into her hand. She's not looking at me again, which breaks my heart. What do I expect though? Why should a woman like her deal with my bullshit—past, present, or future? I told her in the beginning that Ellen will never leave me alone. She won't be happy until she strips me of everything I've ever earned, and she'll never let me love someone else, or more to the point, let them love me.

"I'm so sorry."

Deidre squeezes my fingers, tears springing to her eyes, but she continues to say nothing, her gaze set on something in the distance.

"Who should I call first?"

"I'll call." She opens her palm, and I slide her phone into it. Then I watch as she morphs into Ms. Scott, President of Team Communications.

"Hey. There's been a situation. I need Dr. Simpkins to meet me at Memorial ER as soon as possible."

I'm not sure who she's talking to, but she's all business.

"I'm fine. I'll explain it when I see you next."

A retort I can't hear.

"No, you don't have to come."

She sighs. "Fine."

Hanging up the call, she sends a text to someone else and then another someone and then another. In a ten-minute ambulance ride, she's conducted an unspecified amount of business before she leans back against the gurney and closes her eyes.

All this time, I haven't moved my hand from the empty spot next to her on the bed, waiting until she comes back to me.

As the ambulance pulls into the emergency bay, she rests her fingers on top of mine and, much to my relief, squeezes.

Chapter Twelve
Deidre

Crazy ass bitch. I should have had her arrested months ago when she tried breaking into the facility.

Dr. Simpkins consults with a plastic surgeon and a burn specialist. "You're very lucky you were wearing layers and had people nearby with water to neutralize the acid, otherwise these burns could've been a lot worse."

"Yay. Lucky me," I say dryly, fingering the long strands of hair that burned off my head. I don't exactly know how much of it is gone, but it's enough to warrant a haircut. What kind of haircut, I'm not sure. I'm oddly attracted to the rock star mullet that's cycling through the rebel celebrity circles right now. Maybe it's time to try that?

"Seriously, Deidre. This is slightly worse than a third-degree burn. You should heal fine on your own. We'll give it a few weeks, and if there is any residual scarring, we'll come up with a plan."

"Worse case, maybe a couple of dermabrasion appointments to smooth out the damaged cells," the plastic surgeon tries to reassure me.

"Thanks," I say, wishing they would leave and tell Aggie to come back in. He's freaked—I know it—but thirty minutes ago I didn't have the mental capacity to comfort him. Honestly, right now I still don't, which is why I didn't fight them when they urged him out of the room.

"Baby?" My mom rushes into the room, damn near bowling over the three doctors. "Are you okay?"

"I'm fine." I roll my eyes. "Who called you?"

"Deacon did." Linda Scott, Mama Bear herself, pins Dr. Simpkins in place with a no-nonsense stare. "Is she okay?"

"Yes, ma'am. She's lucky none of it got into her eyes or her mouth. Otherwise, it's like a wicked sunburn or something off a steam iron. Third degree, but nothing requiring a skin graft. We cleaned the affected area and used medicated ointment. We'll check back in a couple days for infection, but as long as she keeps it clean, I expect a full recovery with little to no scarring."

My mom slaps her hand over her mouth at the term *scarring*.

"For fuck's sake. I'm thirty years old and sitting right here." I glance between the doctor I've had since I was a toddler and my mother. The other two doctors seem to know they are no longer needed or wanted, so they excuse themselves and leave the room.

He smiles down at me. "I'll let the nurses know what

you need—ointment, bandages, painkillers, and antibiotics—and we'll have you out of here within an hour."

I look at my mom and give her the chunk of loose hair. "We'll have to get me in with Pablo to fix my hair."

"Oh, baby." My mother's eyes fill with tears.

"Quit it." I shake my head. "It's just hair."

With Dr. Simpkins' departure, the room fills with large, testosterone-laden men, all of whom are wearing way too much aggression for how I'm feeling right now. Usually I'm the hot-head of the family.

Aggie hangs out in the back with one hand shoved in his pocket, the other wrapped in white bandages. I talk past my father and brothers to him. "Are you hurt?"

He shakes his head. "It's nothing."

I look at the men of my family—waiting for the onslaught of berating questions.

What were you doing with my football player, Buster?

He's five years younger than you and he just got divorced, Deidre!

This is a potential scandal for the family and the organization!

"So? You don't have questions for me?"

Deacon shakes his head. "Aggie filled us in. We'll back you one hundred percent on whatever you need, although if she gets out on bail, I'm thinking we will hire private security," my father adds.

Aggie turns his back on me and the rest of the family, his shoulders slumped like they were in my office months ago. Once again, he's broken. "Can you give us a minute?"

My brother Deacon opens his mouth to say something, but I shut him down with an arch of my eyebrow and a slow shake of my head.

He rolls his eyes. "We'll be outside."

"Go buy me a pair of sweats and a coffee, preferably with a shot of Bailey's."

Declan slaps Aggie's shoulder and then turns him to face me, pushing him toward the bed before walking out.

"This isn't your fault," I say.

"Of course it is." He pulls at his hair and paces the edge of the bed. "I knew she wouldn't give up and let me be happy. You warned me this wouldn't be over with a piece of paper. I should have been more careful, especially with you."

"What are you saying?"

"I can't risk something happening to you. I'll never forgive myself for hurting you."

"You didn't hurt me."

"Being with me got you hurt. If she does it again—"

"The only person that bitch is hurting is another inmate, because I can promise you she's never getting out of prison."

Aggie laces his fingers behind his head and closes his eyes. "I can't drag you into my mess."

I stare at him for a moment, my heart breaking as my mind spins, then I shake my head and swing my legs off of the edge of the bed. "No, you're not going to say everything you said to me last night and then push me away today. If you've changed your mind about me, fine, but don't use her as an excuse to do it."

"I meant every word I said—"

"And yet you're ready to walk away?" I say, unable to mask the pain in my voice.

"I understand you're mad—"

"Yes, I'm fucking mad." I pace in my hospital gown, robe, and little booties. This is the one thing I never wanted to do with Aggie—fight.

I mean, I knew it was inevitable. I am me, after all. But he has a lifetime of mental and physical abuse to overcome, and I don't want to set him back in his therapy. I'm a strong female, and the last thing I want to do is bully him.

I don't want to be another version of his ex.

"I'm angry with myself for not taking care of her months ago in the way I knew I'd have to. I was gentle because of my feelings for you, even though I knew a soft approach wouldn't work on her. I'm livid with her for being a delusional nut bag who thinks she still deserves you after everything she's done. And I'm pissed at you for taking it from her all of these years, thus enabling the crazy delusion she lives in. And now I'm really pissed at you for whispering words of love and adoration to me all night, only to recant them in the face of... what?"

"An acid attack, Deidre." He moves to cup my face and then pulls his hand away. "A fucking acid attack. What's next? She gets her hand on a gun?"

"She's going to prison. She can fantasize about shooting me from her eight by six cell." My mother and

Declan walk in with a shopping bag, their gazes bouncing between us. I sigh. "You should leave. I have plenty of help here."

I grab the bag and walk into the bathroom, shouting as the door closes behind me. "Find that damn nurse so we can get out of here."

Eight hours later, I'm sitting in front of my fireplace wearing fuzzy velour yoga pants and an oversized sweatshirt, a large decaf coffee with two shots of Bailey's in my hand. My family left me alone hours ago, their self-preservation kicking in once my mood to snip at them overwhelmed their concern and love for me.

I hate the way I kicked Aggie out of the hospital room and my last words to him. He needs time to decide what he wants and if it's me. I knew that going into last night, but then he said so many sweet things—things I desperately want to believe—I let myself get swept into the delusion that we were starting our future. That's my fault.

But now I don't know what to do. Anyone else, I'd be a bitch and move on with my life, but I can't do that to Aggie. I care too much about him.

I hear a truck door slam before a heavy hand lands on my door. My gaze is on the foyer as Aggie pushes inside, his big body filling the threshold, his eyes instantly finding me. I set my coffee down and stand up, but say nothing—because I'm not sure what to say. The words *I'm sorry* sit on my tongue, but I'm not. I didn't say anything I didn't mean.

The only thing I'm sorry for is pushing him away.

"I'm sorry." We speak at the same time.

He moves across my living room with speed and grace, stopping in front of me. "I was scared and not thinking straight."

"Me too." I nod, a rogue tear slipping out of my eye.

He reaches for me, tentatively putting his fingers against my jaw, wiping away the tear. "How do you feel?"

"I'm fine. How's your hand?"

"I'll be able to play next Sunday." Aggie rubs his thumb over my lips and lowers his forehead against mine.

"Good."

"This was not how I planned to spend the day." He gives me a sad excuse for a smile.

"Which part?"

"All of it. I thought we'd grab coffee, eat pastries, and then crawl back into bed all day."

I chuckle. "That sounds nice. How'd it go at the police department?"

"The DA will call us early next week. Meanwhile, the cop told me there was no way she'll be released on bail before her first hearing, and considering the violent nature of her attack, he doubts she'll get bail no matter what."

I smile and duck my head, completely confident she won't be getting out soon. We know the DA. She's a family friend, and we've already informed her of today's events. "That's good."

Aggie sits down on my couch and pulls me into his lap. "Can we pick up where we were disrupted this morning?"

"I have coffee and pastries in my kitchen."

"I brought leftover lasagna, which Rev is probably digging into right now."

I giggle, resting the right side of my face against his chest and kissing his jaw. "Go get your dog and rescue my dinner."

Aggie claims my lips, his touch gentle on my face, his fingers insistent everywhere else. "Okay, but when I come back, I'm starting with dessert."

"Am I the dessert?"

"All day, every day."

Chapter Thirteen
Aggie

Three weeks have gone by, and I'm the happiest I've ever been. Deidre and I spend a couple nights every week together, but otherwise have kept our relationship on the down low. It's not that we're hiding it, we're just not flaunting it until after the season and Ellen's trial.

In the end, we both agree it's for the best.

Speaking of which, Ellen's still in jail. The judge emphatically denied her request for bail. She's had her lawyer, not Mr. Peterson, contact my lawyer multiple times, requesting I visit her in jail. So far, I've said no every time. Eventually, I'll have to see her—whether that be in a courtroom or with plexiglass between us, I don't know. While I'm angry at her for what she's done, I mostly feel sorry for her. She's never going to be happy if she doesn't let go of the past and get the help she desperately needs.

"What do you have planned for tonight?" Devlin asks

after another amazing win. We clinched our division last week, so it's smooth sailing into the playoffs from here. Still, there are stats to achieve and records to break, so we'll play our hardest every game until the season is over.

"I think I'll chill at home tonight, maybe decorate the tree or something," I say. It's days before Christmas, and although Devlin and Declan know about Deidre, we don't talk about my relationship. From Declan's perspective, I don't think he really wants to know. The whole 'that's my sister and best friend" conundrum. Devlin, well, he still hasn't told me about his relationship, so in turn, he doesn't ask about mine. At some point we'll talk —I'm sure of it—because nothing matters to me more than my friends' happiness.

"Yeah, me too," he says.

"Aggie." Greg walks up as we're grabbing our shower stuff. "When you're done, they want you upstairs."

I frown. Thirteen weeks ago, this ominous note would've put a boulder in my belly, but if there were problems brewing, Deidre would've given me a heads up. "What's going on?"

Greg shrugs. "I don't know. Errand boy just knocked on the door and gave me this note, and said to hurry."

I take the note and open it. "Come meet your fans in my private box, room 401."

Assuming this note is a bunch of euphemisms, I'm unable to stop the cheesy grin spreading my lips across my face.

I wash up quickly, get dressed, and am in the elevator before anyone can sideline me with a conversation.

Deidre's standing outside her private box, looking beautiful in a pair of skin-tight jeans and a Rangers jersey. Then I notice the numbers. She's wearing my jersey, and a possessive pride fills my heart and infuses my soul. Blood moves south, but I push it aside considering she's standing outside of her suite with the door closed while talking to a few die-hard fans as they say their goodbyes. A few of them recognize me, which almost never happens, and congratulate me on another amazing game.

"Thanks." I shake a couple of hands, but my eyes keep coming back to the number on her jersey.

She smiles and gives me a knowing wink.

Only after they're gone does Deidre step into my chest and kiss me softly. "Don't be mad."

My mind is already on other things, so it takes a few seconds for her words to register. "Mad about what?"

"I'm not trying to run your life, and I swear this is the last time I put my nose into your business."

I take a step back. "What did you do?"

"Understand, I did this because I care about you." She bites her lip and opens the door.

The first thing I see is my mother who, upon laying eyes on me, bursts into tears and jumps up from her seat. "My baby!"

Quickly, I clock every member of my family and then some—an in-law and a niece and nephew I've yet to meet. "Holy hell."

"There's my son." My father stands, his face contorting with rarely displayed emotion.

"Mom? Dad?" I stumble into the room, the shock of

seeing them after so many years tightening bands across my chest.

"We are so proud of you." My mom rushes me as if no time at all has passed, sliding her arms around my waist.

"You are amazing on the field. The guys at the bar are tired of hearing me talk about you every week." My father slaps me on the shoulder.

"You got big, bro." My sister stands with a toddler on her hip.

My brain engages. The reality of the scene before me unfolds to tell an unreal story, one I couldn't figure out how to bring to fruition on my own.

Deidre brought my family to me. Every one of them is here in Colorado with me. I wrap my arms around my mom, squeezing her tight like a lifeline as tears spill down my cheeks. "I can't believe you're here."

"Ms. Scott said you wanted us to come to a game, and then she made it near impossible to say no." My father chuckles.

I glance over my shoulder at Deidre, who watches us from the doorway with a sweet smile on her face and unshed tears in her eyes. "You did this?"

She smiles. "You have the box for the next couple hours, and I made dinner reservations at Castilla's Reserve downtown for seven. There's a car waiting for the family when the time comes to leave the stadium. Otherwise, take your time catching up with your family. I'll have a security guard standing outside, in case you want to take them on a tour or something before you go."

Nodding at my family, she ducks her head. "It was nice to meet all of you. If you need anything, you have my number."

Deidre flashes me a coy smile and then slips out of the room.

"I'll be right back." I pull out of my mom's arms and chase Deidre out of the room, calling over my shoulder at my family. "Give me five minutes."

"Where are you going?"

Deidre stops before the elevators. "I'm giving you time alone with your family. Are you mad?"

"Of course not. I have a million questions, but I'm not mad." I glance around and yank her into what turns out to be a storage closet. Pulling her flush against my body, I cup her face and shake my head. "Why'd you do that?"

She shrugs. "I want you to be happy."

"I am happy—with you."

"Yes, baby, and I'm happy with you, but I want you to have everything, which includes your family—who, by the way, love you very much." The tears she's been holding back slide down her cheeks.

I swallow the lump in my throat and use my thumb to swipe at the tears. Screw it, I'm going for it. "I love you, Deidre."

Her lips part and a small gasp escapes as her eyebrows shoot up in surprise.

I close my eyes and claim her lips, taking away the awkwardness of my proclamation, or at least hide from it.

I shouldn't have said it.

It's too soon.

And yet I feel it with every fiber of my being. We kiss until we're breathless. Her fingers dig into my shoulders as my hands slip under her ass and pull her legs up around my waist. "Are you coming to dinner?"

"I hadn't planned on it. I thought I'd give you a couple of nights with your family and let you celebrate Christmas together."

"What if I want you by my side?" I press my forehead against hers and open my eyes to find her aqua eyes vibrant in the fluorescent overhead lighting.

"Then I will be by your side." She bites her lip. "Because I love you too."

Epilogue
Aggie - Three Months Later...

If your team makes it to the championship game, the season spans six months, starting with the first preseason game in August. If healthy at the end of the season, we get approximately ten weeks off to heal, relax, and vacation before the next season's training camp starts.

I'm spending two of those weeks in Maui with Deidre at an oceanfront villa with a private beach.

Two weeks of her wearing nothing but a bikini, sarong, and a smile, except when my family is here for five days.

Now that we've reconnected, I want to give them all the things I couldn't while married to Ellen. My parents have barely enough to keep a roof over their heads, the land they live on worth very little, but somehow they've always kept the heat on and food on the table. When I brought Deidre home to see where I grew up, I'm ashamed to say I was embarrassed. We come from very different worlds, and I was afraid of how she would view me after seeing my childhood home.

She exceeded my expectations, never once making my mother feel self-conscious about her home. Then, privately, she suggested that while my parents would never take a new home from me—something I offered over dinner on the first night—maybe I could pay a contractor to come in and do some much needed repairs to the roof, foundation, water heater, and furnace. Thankfully, my father agreed after some gentle coaxing.

I'm throwing in a new kitchen, too, when he's not paying attention. My mother loves to cook, and she deserves it.

My sister, Jennifer, has done a little better than my parents, moving out of Rizona to a place with opportunity. She's three years younger than me and moved to San Antonio after high school, where she got a job and an apartment, and eventually met her husband, David. They have a two-year-old named Jason and an apartment on the north side. He works at the airport pulling down decent money while she works as a CNA hoping to go to school to become an RN someday.

I'll make that happen this fall.

I'm flying them all out for a long weekend and putting them up in the bungalow next to ours.

"What time is it?" Deidre comes out of the bedroom in a white bikini which makes her skin shimmer a golden hue.

My gaze caresses every inch of her. She's beautiful—

inside and out—and takes my breath away every time she enters the room.

"It's time to sit on my lap." I flash her a cheesy grin when she brings her eyes up to meet mine and slowly shakes her head.

"I was thinking you might want to swim before your family gets here."

"One, they won't be here for another two hours. Two, they're going to be exhausted when they get here because it'll be past midnight back home. Three, we can swim with them, but the things I want to do to you right now are not family friendly."

She giggles. "The things you did to me this morning weren't family friendly either."

"Exactly. I need to get it all in before they get here." I slip my hand between her legs, stroking the cotton barrier between me and her hot pussy.

As always, Deidre spreads her legs for me, granting me access to her body whenever I want, with no stipulations attached. She doesn't use sex as a bargaining chip with me, enjoying my body as much as I do hers, initiating as often or more than I do. She demonstrates her love for me physically, as well as verbally and emotionally. I've never felt on edge with her, or unsure how she feels about me or our relationship.

With Deidre, I know we are solid, and after experiencing her love, I know Ellen never really loved me.

"Does that mean you don't plan on touching me for five days?" She raises her brow and uses her hand to stop my fingers from pushing her bikini bottoms aside.

"No. It means there will be a lot more stolen moments and fewer lap dances."

Deidre grabs my hand and places it on the top of the couch. "You want another lap dance?"

I nod. "Yes."

She climbs off my lap and grabs my hand, pulling me to my feet. "Come with me, sailor."

We walk out to the lanai hand in hand, the sun setting on the horizon over the ocean. She pushes me toward one of the lounge chairs, pushing the arms down on the sides and setting the back at a forty-five degree angle. "Get comfortable. I'll put on some music."

Before she walks away, I pull her into my chest and capture her lips, kissing her softly and slipping my tongue against hers until a growl reverberates in my throat. Blood rushes to my cock and I'm ready to forgo the lap dance and take her right here and now.

She knows—she always knows—and pushes off my chest with a coy smile. "You asked for a lap dance, and that's what you're going to get."

I sit down in the chair and adjust myself, grinning like a loon as music plays overhead and the hot tub jets and lights turn on—both of which are controlled with a flick of a button near the sliding glass door.

Deidre uses her sarong as a prop, dancing circles around me before stepping over my legs, her back to me; her round ass shaking in my face. She wraps her fingers around my thighs and drops low, grinding her pussy against my board shorts-clad cock.

"Ohhh," I groan, my fingers digging into the soft

wood of the lounge chair. Although I still haven't visited a strip club—I never plan to, honestly—Deidre has schooled me in all the rules and etiquette. Meaning, I keep my hands to myself.

But it's so damn hard when she's touching me.

Smiling, she leans back and lays her head on my chest. "Feel good, baby?"

"Yes."

"You want more?" She kisses my jaw. When we play like this, I'm not allowed to touch her, but she's allowed to do whatever she wants to me. She teases until I can't take anymore, and when I get to that point, I have to say *Champagne Room*, which means all bets are off.

I had no idea I liked being teased because I had no idea what having a healthy sexual relationship felt like. Turns out, I love it—when it's by Deidre and only her.

"I want your pussy in my face." I grin at the momentary shock on her face. Another thing I've discovered with Deidre is that I have a filthy mouth. Again, only with her.

"You didn't say Champagne Room."

"I don't plan on using my hands."

"Oh, really?" She slides her hand between us, pulling my cock free of my shorts, kneading and stroking and rubbing the head against her bikini bottoms.

"No hands, just my tongue and mouth." I suck in my breath and lick my lips, taunting her. "So I do not need to say Champagne Room."

She pushes off of me and stands up, pulling the strings of her bikini bottoms until the entire thing falls as a limp piece of fabric to the ground. Then she does the same with her top, her skin glowing from the hot tub lights and the near dark sky.

"No hands," she warns.

Once again, she straddles my legs and backs up until her sweet arousal touches my lips. I lick her deep, plunging my tongue inside her sweet cunt as she wraps her fingers around me and strokes me in earnest. I fuck her with my tongue and suck her clit into my mouth until her legs shake and she begs me to slide my cock deep inside her.

Chuckling, I tease, "Are you calling Champagne Room?"

This will be a first.

"Yes."

"Let's hear it, baby."

"Champagne Room! Please, Aggie, fuck me."

I wrap my fingers around her hips and guide her down on my cock, both of us moaning our pleasure into the still night. She leans back against my chest, her fingers gripping my thighs as she rides me. With my lips on her throat, I wrap one hand over her breasts, the other going to her clit to push her over the edge. It takes seconds to turn her into a quivering pile of need, her orgasm crashing over while her pussy clamps down and squeezes me for everything I have to give her.

But I'm not done yet.

As soon as she releases me, I push her to her feet and bend her over the hot tub to take her hard and fast from behind.

"Oh, yes!" she pants, slapping her palm against the lining. "I love you so much."

Those three words send cum shooting from my balls every time. I come hard, my fingers digging into her hips before I slump over her back and sprinkle kisses on her shoulder. "I love you too, babe."

Second Epilogue
Deidre - Two years later...

"There's my pretty birthday girl." I take my niece, Annabelle, or Belle for short, from Amelia's arms and pepper her chunky cheeks with kisses. She has a beautiful smile and makes my insides twist whenever she flashes it my way.

Aggie walks up behind me and spreads his big hand over the small of my back while resting his chin on my shoulder and wagging his brow at the little girl.

She giggles.

He always makes her smile, just like her auntie.

Aggie presses a kiss to my neck and then zerberts her cheek, causing her to cackle in delight. "You want something to drink, babe?"

"I'll take the usual."

He nods and wiggles his fingers in Belle's face who tries to capture them with her chunky hands.

We've been together for over two years and although we sleep together every night he's not on the road, we still don't live together. After the life he lived with Ellen, I didn't want him to feel trapped with me by insisting he give up his first and only bachelor pad.

It's a simple of his freedom, if nothing else.

I try to tell myself it's okay. The fact that we don't live together—aren't engaged or married after two years—is not a reflection of our dedication to each other, but sometimes I wonder if it will ever happen.

I know Aggie is my last love. To be honest, he's my only love. Foolishly, I thought I had been in love before, but what I had with my exes is nothing compared to the all-consuming need and devotion I felt with Aggie our first night together.

And I'm confident he feels the same.

And yet, I'm not sure he's interested in taking the next step. Maybe he never wants to be married again. Can I blame him?

I take a seat with Belle in my lap, watching Declan with his seven-year-old son Danny play on the giant swing set in their backyard. Deacon stands beside him at the same time my sister-in-law London comes out of the house with a freshly changed Zachary in her arms, my other sister-in-law Amelia by her side. My mother Linda and Amelia's mother Vivian busy themselves inside while my father Daniel talks to Greg McMillan, our offensive coordinator and Vivian's new boyfriend.

We really do like to keep it all within the Rangers family.

Aggie comes back with a vodka tonic full of citrus slices and sets it in front of me on the table, once again leaning down to kiss me and then the baby. "Here you go, beautiful."

"Thank you."

"Is there anything else I can get you?"

"You don't have to wait on me, Aggie. Go hang out with the boys."

As soon as he walks away, London sits on one side of me while Amelia sits in the chair besides me. "The babies do love their auntie Deidre."

I grin. "And auntie Deidre loves her babies."

There's a momentary silence which brings my head up to catch London and Amelia sharing a knowing look. I narrow my eyes but keep my voice light for the babe in my arms. "What was that look?"

Amelia shrugs. She works for me and we spent an inordinate amount of time together throughout the workday and steal London for lunch at least once a week. After a lifetime of being the only girl, it's nice to have a couple of sisters. Still, that they have secrets raises my hackles. I'm used to being the one that knows everything.

"We were wondering what's going on with you and Aggie?" London says casually, as if she is asking about the weather.

"What do you mean?"

"Well, you've been together for two years now. Are you going to move-in together? Get married? Have babies of your own? What's next on the Daggie train?"

"Daggie?" My head snaps up, and I cast both of them an incredulous look. Belle, who just dozed off, stirs in my arms. I lower my voice and hiss as pleasantly as possible, "Where the F did Daggie spawn from?"

"You don't like it?" Amelia giggles. "We thought it up while trolling the gossip rags for any hits on any of our players. It was that or Agdre, but that's kind of awful."

"Don't worry, D. We made them up for us too." London smiles. "For Deacon and me, it's Leacon—which sounds like a cut-rate car maker—or Dondon. Either way, they're bad."

"And for Declan and me, it's Dames, Delia, or Ameclan—none of which flow nearly as well as Daggie."

I roll my eyes. "You two have too much time on your hands."

"So?" Amelia leans forward and lowers her voice. "Are you two talking about what's next?"

I shrug casually, but my tone has a bit of a bite to it. "Why does there have to be something next? We're completely content with our current arrangement. Why do I have to be married to prove I am completely devoted to him?"

Amelia blanches, her mouth opening and closing quickly.

"You don't." London sighs. "Honestly, I never thought I'd get married. I mean, I don't know that being married changes my feelings for Deacon. Although, I will admit, on a subconscious level, knowing we are married fills me with a security I wouldn't have thought necessary or possible."

I narrow my eyes. I can't help it. She picks at my base insecurity without even knowing it. "We all know couples where a piece of paper means absolute dick. Aggie himself understands how marriage only means something if both halves of the couple will put the work into the relationship."

Amelia reaches out and brushes her finger over her daughter's cheek. "We're not trying to pick at you. It's just we see how you are with your nieces and nephews and know you'd be an amazing mom."

"And Aggie would be a fantastic dad." London adds.

"But if that's not what you want, that's fine, too. I enjoy having someone I can trust to babysit." Amelia flashes me a friendly smile.

"And, to be honest—" London hedges "—although our weddings were beautiful, we know yours will be the best of all."

"Maybe you can throw a party where we force our men to dress up with us?" Amelia's smile grows wider.

"Ah." I nod knowingly, tamping down all my hurt and jumbled up feelings—for now. "You want a fancy party? I can do that without getting married. Easy."

Amelia and London seem to know it's time to drop the subject, lest they bring out my president of communications side where I shut shit down without niceties. I give it a few minutes and then gingerly hand Belle over to Amelia, excusing myself for a bathroom break. Grabbing my ice cold drink, I down half of it as I walk into Declan and Amelia's kid friendly house complete with playrooms and framed crayon art.

I'm staring at a collage of wedding photographs near the bathroom when Aggie enters the hallway.

"Everything okay?" He steps behind me and slides his hands around my waist, pulling me back into his broad chest.

"Everything's fine." I say with a clipped tone I don't mean.

His arms tense around me. "Doesn't sound fine."

Taking a deep breath, I turn in his arms and smile up at him. "I love you."

The crease in his brow deepens as wariness sets in. "I love you, too."

His brown eyes search mine as I say nothing. I mean, what am I supposed to say? I thought I was fine not being married, but am I truly?

My big, beautiful man presses his lips together and frames my face with his large, warm hands. "What's wrong, Deidre? Tell me."

"It's nothing. It's stupid."

"Not to me, it's not."

I sigh and sag a little more into his embrace. "Amelia and London were asking me what's next for us, and I didn't have an answer. You know how I hate not having an answer."

His lips quirk. "Yes, I know."

I rest my forehead against his sternum. "Are you happy?"

"The happiest I've ever been." His deep voice vibrates his chest.

"Me too." Nodding, I keep my cheek pressed against his heart.

"Are you sure?" He strokes my hair.

I pull my head back and look up into his eyes with the biggest smile I can make, the one I only give to him. "Absolutely."

Aggie

Just as I lean down to claim her lips, Declan comes around the corner with Deacon behind him. "Ewww. No making out in my hallway."

Deidre narrows her eyes and shoots him a look full of playful venom. "You're lucky that's all I'm doing to him in your hallway. If I knew you were coming, I'd have gotten down on my kne—"

"Lalalalalala." Both of her brothers say, one with his hand over his eyes, the other with his hands over his ears. If I didn't know better, I'd say they've practiced that.

Rolling her eyes, Deidre rises on her tiptoes and gives me a chaste peck on the lips. "I'm going to see what's going on with the food."

She leaves me in the hallway to fend for myself. In the beginning, I was nervous about showing her affection in front of them. They are not only her brothers, but my teammate, best friend, and boss. But she put an end to that quickly and doubles down whenever they try to give her shit.

"Come with us." Declan motions to the garage.

"What are we doing?" I ask as I follow them into the massive four-car garage to see a new king-cab truck parked where his Jeep used to be. "Nice. When did you get that?"

"Last week. I need it to tow the new thirty-three foot camper I'm picking up tomorrow. Danny loves the lake and the woods, so I hope to get some camping done next spring and summer." Declan slaps his palm down on my shoulder. "I'm tell you two now, so you can get your shit together and assemble your own camping caravans. As the kids get older, it'll be fun to have the families go out together."

Frowning, I shake my head. "I don't see Deidre down with sleeping in a camper."

"Trust me. My new rig is a luxury apartment. Yours will be too."

I bite my lip. There's so much to do before I have to worry about whether Deidre wants to sleep in a camper. Unspoken things between us creep up more and more lately, and I've been dragging my feet and avoiding the conversation because the last thing I want to do is risk losing what we currently have.

But something tells me we're coming to a critical crossroads in our relationship. If we aren't moving forward, then what are we working toward?

"Do you have any outdoor blankets I can borrow?" I ask, seemingly out of nowhere.

Declan arches his brow. "Yeah. Why?"

"I think I'll take Deidre up to the mountains to talk under the stars after the party."

"Ewww. You're not going to have sex with my sister on my blankets."

My expression turns placid.

I don't talk about sex.

I never have.

And he knows this.

Deacon smacks Declan across the back of the head and then shoves him aside. "Grab the man some blankets and a foam pad, jackass."

Declan rolls his eyes and pulls a tub off the shelf, handing it to me. "Everything you need to outfit the back of your truck."

"Maybe you should pack a cooler while you are at it?"

"Yeah. I can grab you a bottle of champagne and a couple of flutes." Declan grins, his eyes bouncing between me and his brother. "Is this it? Is tonight the night?"

"What?" Deacon asks.

I shake my head. "I don't know."

"What!" Deacon presses.

"Too many months ago, Ags asked me about a jeweler. I haven't seen him wearing any new bling, and Deidre hasn't shown off any jewelry, so I assume he's looking at engagement rings." Declan crosses his arms over his chest and leans back against his new truck with a satisfied smirk on his face.

"Really?" Deacon nods his approval.

I growl my annoyance and snatch the bin from Declan, carrying it through the side door to my truck. We spend the next couple hours eating and celebrating a one-year-old as she smashes white frosting in her chubby little hands, and then finally it's time to go.

My heart is in my throat as we drive off the property and I take a right onto Hwy-24 up the mountain pass.

"Where are you going?" Deidre glances around when she realizes I'm not heading toward either of our homes.

"I want to show you something." I reach across the console and slide my hand on her thigh.

Deidre leans into me, mimicking my position by placing her delicate hand on my leg. Her explicit trust in me is one of the many things I treasure about her.

It takes about twenty minutes to get to my spot up the mountain overlooking the city and there are approximately twenty minutes before sunset. I back my truck up into the tiny dirt pull-off cut between the trees just deep enough to get my front end off the road. That's why no one stops here, because they can't figure out how to park their massive off-road vehicles in the tiny spot. And yet, with the trees, we're completely secluded from the mountain road.

It's my favorite place in the whole world.

"Where are we, babe?" Deidre frowns.

"Come on." I tilt my head and encourage her to get out. Jumping into the bed, I spread out the foam roll and blankets and then offer her my hand, hauling her up with me. We lean against the back and face the valley and mountain peaks ahead of us, the sun just about to kiss the top. I wrap my arm around her shoulders and pull her close, throwing one blanket over our legs. "When I first move here with Ellen, I found this spot. It was the one place I could go to hide from her, from everything. It's my safe haven when things get to be too much. I haven't felt the need to come up here in almost two years."

She looks to the horizon, sighing contently as the sun dips below the mountain peak. "It's peaceful."

"Yeah." I bury my face into her neck, inhaling her sweet fragrance, and gathering up my courage. "Do you think... I mean... shit."

Deidre snorts and wraps her arms around mine. "Do I think shit?"

"No. This is going to sound dumb and antiquated, but there was a time when the man's role was to provide for his woman, but let's be honest, I'm never going to be able to give you better than you can give yourself."

She sits up, pulls out of my grasp, and turns to look at me. "What are you talking about? Money?"

"Yeah." I cast my gaze down. "I know you love me, as I love you, but why would you marry me when I have nothing I can give you?"

"Marry you?" Her breath hitches as she takes my hands and pulls my eyes up to hers. "Are you asking me to marry you?"

"God, I am really messing this up." I shake my head. "Deidre, I've wanted to marry you since our first trip to Maui, and over the last two years, I've thought of a dozen different ways to propose."

"Then why haven't you?"

"Because I can't provide for you better than you can provide for yourself. How am I supposed to go to your father and ask for your hand when I know I can't do that basic thing?" I hold my hand up when her lips part to protest. "I know you don't care about that. I know it. But it's been ingrained in me since I was a kid that a husband provides for his wife."

She narrows her eyes. "Ingrained by who? Ellen?"

"Yes." I blush, thankful the sky has darkened enough to hide my red cheeks.

"I have so much I could say about that, but it's not important right now." Deidre shifts to her knees and then straddles my thighs, wrapping her arm around my neck. I can't help but slide my palms up her quads until I nestle my thumbs near her pussy. There is something addictive about the way this woman loves to touch me as much as I love to touch her. "You know what you give me, baby. In the last two years, you've provided me with support in every other way. No, I don't need your money, but my heart, my mind, my spirit need you. They'd shrivel up and die without you. You've shown me love and affection, safety and surety, happiness and friendship—the likes of which I never thought I'd know. You take care of my heart, my mind, and my body."

"Did you ever doubt that I wanted forever with you?" I brush her hair back from her face and cup her cheek lovingly.

"No." She shakes her head. "I've never doubted your commitment to me, and yet, we're in the same place we were two years ago. I wanted to ask you to move in, but I didn't want to take away the security of having your own place. Sometimes I worry that I'm acting like Ellen—possessive or demanding—and the last thing I ever want to do is remind you of her. That's why I haven't pushed for the next thing."

"What is the next thing?" The horizon is a light purple now as the sun dips its head below the mountain and an instant chill touches the air. I pull her closer so she's straddling my cock, which stirs in her proximity, and put her lips within kissing distance. I love this woman more than I can comprehend. I didn't know a love this consuming was possible. It's the kind that makes your heart hurt a little bit as it thumps in your chest.

"Living together." Deidre leans forward and presses her lips to mine with her fingers dug into the waistband of my pants. "If you want to, you can move in with me. Or we can find a house we like and buy it together. Or, if it's so important to you, you can buy a house and I'll move in with you. Either way, even though we've completely opened our homes to each other, I love the idea of truly living together and making one happy home."

"You know I don't care where I live, as long as I have you to come home to night after night. I don't need a man cave or my own space, and I couldn't care less about the opulence of my home. I just need you." I press my thumbs into the juncture between her thighs and flex my fingers, pulling her even closer.

Deidre's eyes darken, and she tightens her grip. "Then move in with me. Give up the condo and live with me—permanently."

"Done." I claim her lips in an all-consuming kiss, my brain lighting up with images of our future. I'm going to ask her father's permission this week. I'll propose with the ring in my center console next week. Maybe we'll start a family, maybe we won't. I don't really care either way. Sure, I melt when I see her with a baby in her arms. And yes, the idea of her swollen with my child wakes something primal within me. But I think we can have a fulfilling life as a childless couple, doting on our nieces and nephews, too. Plus, the selfish part of me doesn't want to share her, although I'll keep that desire under wraps.

"Aggie?" Deidre trails kisses along my jaw and up to my ear as I knead her jean covered thighs. Damn, I wish she had worn a skirt today. I would play with her clit right now.

"Yes, baby?"

"Are you going to make love to me under the stars?"

"Absolutely, and then again when we get home."

"Home." She murmurs as I slip my tongue between her lips again and roll her to her back, the two of us stretched out under the night sky.

The night air is still, the road mostly desolate as I make love to my future wife. Although our love and commitment to each other was never in question, something about having this conversation with our future mapped out in front of us fills me with a deeper peace I hadn't known I was missing.

This is what a loving relationship looks like, and I will never give it up.

Luckily for me, Deidre will never give me up, either.

Also by Kameron Claire

Want more **Witty** Tongues, **Wicked** Needs, & **Wild** Deeds?

<u>Hollywood Lights (Pre-Order)</u>

** Billionaire Romance **

Show Time (Securing Selyne)

Money Shot

Three Shot

Martini Shot

Long Shot

<u>Veteran K9 Team</u>

** Military Romance **

Mine to Cherish

Mine to Crave

Mine to Possess

Mine to Adore

Mine to Covet

Mine to Worship

Mine to Protect

Mine to Treasure

Hot Nights with the Boss

** Forbidden Office / Age-Gap Romances **

Dating the Boss

Flirting with the Boss

Teasing the Boss

Tempting the Boss

Rangers Football

** Sports Romance **

Play Action Fake

Quarterback Sneak

Personal Foul

Two-Point Conversion

Red Zone

Man to Man Coverage

Short Story Collections and Bundles

Animal Attraction 4-Story Collection

Vegas Nights 4-Story Collection

Last Stand Saloon 4-Story Collection

Instalove Bundle

About the Author

USA Today Bestselling Author Kameron Claire writes stories with witty tongues, wicked needs, and wild deeds. Her books emphasize strong female leads and the protective alpha males who know how to love and support kick-ass, take-charge women. Many of her books contain military veterans, boss babes, gentle but dominant men, and goofy K9 hijinks.

Find her everywhere via linktr.ee/kameronclaire
Signed Paperbacks and discounted eBook bundles are available exclusively on her store
Subscribe to the Witty, Wicked & Wild community and read all her books online for as little as $5 a month.

www.ingramcontent.com/pod-product-compliance
Lightning Source LLC
Chambersburg PA
CBHW030143010826
48973CB00002B/703